TWO LARGE WHISKEYS

John Hurley

First published in Great Britain

All paper used in the printing of this book has been made from wood grown in managed, sustainable forests.

ISBN13: 978-1-78003-762-2

Printed and bound in the UK

Penpress is an imprint of
Author Essentials
4 The Courtyard
South Street
Falmer
E Sussex
BN1 9PQ

A catalogue record of this book is available from the British Library

Cover design by Jacqueline Abromeit

CONTENTS

INFANCY AND CHILDHOOD

My name is Patrick Eades. I came into the world in 1935. It was not headline news and never made it to births, marriages and deaths in the national press. However it was important to my parents. I was the first born and like all parents, I suppose they thought I was special.

Most normal thing in the world they say. I have never thought that. We come through a channel that was badly designed for such an event. After spending months cocooned and floating peacefully in our mother's womb, we come on this earth and the first thing we receive is a slap on the arse from the midwife. They say it is to help us take our first breaths. I wonder; maybe it's to prepare us for the harsh realities of life. In my case I was lucky. I was always treated with tenderness and love. The wonders of parenthood, they had no pre-natal classes, and relied on natural instincts.

Our family expanded rapidly and I soon had one sister and a brother. They seemed to come into my life with great stealth and secrecy. Most children in that era were born in the beds they were conceived in. Neighbours took hold of the younger children and the midwife arrived, usually on a bike with high handle bars, and a basket attached, she also carried a black bag. As a child I knew there was a connection between the basket and the fact that when she left there was always a squalling baby left behind.

Sex education at that time consisted of winks, nods and overheard whispered conversations. Children seldom dwell on these matters but there was one thing, even as a child, that was impossible to ignore, that was the war.

We became the proud possessors of a radio. It dominated the corner of one room and I felt my father was the only one who had the skill to operate it. It was large and brown and was powered by two square glass, wet batteries. It had stretched hessian cloth at the front and two large knobs, one to find the station and the other for fine tuning.

We were plagued with bad reception, especially when the charge began to die in the batteries. Neighbours gathered to hear the nine o'clock news. There seemed to be a lot of whistling and crackling noises coming from it. Silence from the listeners was important and my mother always eyeballed me with her index finger in front of her lips. People that were far removed from the conflict had a tendency after the news to rubbish the people engaged in it.

About this time my godfather came to visit. He brought me a red pedal motor car that must have made me the envy of my peers. He held a senior position in the army and had a staff car and driver. I recall the driver had a smart uniform with highly polished boots, and the staff car glinted in the early morning sun in front of our house. When they left, a photograph of our dead beloved leader Michael Collins hung next to the Sacred Heart over our mantelpiece. Funny I can never remember playing with the toy car or where it ended up.

My godfather had spent time in prison during the War of Independence and of course, that did wonders for his career, when things changed. He died of a heart attack shortly after that. I could not really grasp what death was about. I knew it was serious; I saw the tears and felt the sadness but then as now people do not dwell on it. My aunty grasped my hand at the funeral. There were lines of men in uniform and a man in a dark suit seemed to go on forever about him

Starting primary school opened up a new world for me. Mary Horan, my first teacher, was a large dignified grey haired lady. She rode a bicycle that seemed to have an inordinate amount of punctures. Always carrying her rosary beads, she prayed incessantly to St Christopher. Even then I thought, if he is the patron saint of travellers, why does she get so many punctures? Heavily built and wearing long voluminous dresses, when she was cycling you could just make out the bottom halves of the bicycle wheels. Slacks for ladies in her position would have been out of the question, so frequently her dresses got snagged in the chain. She must have had a good supply of black dresses because frequently, full of piety and patience, she sat and repaired torn hems in the classroom.

"Things are sent to try us children, and I find it helpful to offer up my crosses to God."

The living and the dead were mentioned in her prayers and especially the ragamuffins she was surrounded by. Never marrying and living with her bachelor brother, they both strongly believed in fairies. Her brother especially had frequent meetings with the little people. Priests and head teachers tried to dissuade her from filling our heads with tales of banshees and headless horsemen driving through the countryside on dark nights. One of her tales I can remember quite well:

"Look, as true as I am sitting here, when my brother was coming home on Friday night the pony stopped before the bridge. He stuck his two front legs out straight and would not lead or drive. Eoghan said the harness and draught chains were vibrating on the cart with the shivering of the animal. The hair was standing on his neck, and the next thing, the coach came across the bridge. Four horses and iron bands on the wheels. He could see the sparks from them on the road and the horses snorting as if they were in mortal terror."

"Did he get home safe, Miss?"

"Oh he did. When the coach had gone the pony came back to his senses, but Eoghan was pale as a candle when he came into the house."

Speaking Gaelic fluently with a musical soft voice, we were all instilled with a love of our native tongue when it was starting to go out of fashion. My best friend piped up in class one day.

"Miss, my uncle says you do a great job with us children, especially with the Irish, because a country without a language is like a woman without knickers."

There was a silence and the rest of the class looked at the floor. After a while she stammered "Why?"

"Because she is defenceless, Miss."

"I will speak to your uncle," Mary Horan, red-faced and disconcerted answered in a moment of high drama, with a classroom full of children trying to hide their giggles.

During the absence of the head teacher, she sometimes had to take charge. Her rosary beads never left her hands on those days. Despite her best efforts chaos and confusion prevailed. Mr Owen's older boys ran riot. Paper darts flew, numerous conversations were carried on, and ink was spilt in large quantities. She appealed to our non-existent better natures, as her sweet and loving nature could not instil discipline. She warned us of the day of reckoning when the head returned and introduced the cane once more. Intuition told us she would not snitch, a classic example of kindness taken as weakness.

At seven, having reached the use of reason, we stood in a little circle around Mary Horan. This was our preparation for our first confession and communion. I know I was apprehensive. She seemed to gaze straight at me and her rosary beads were clasped in her hands.

"You know we are all sinners, you, me, and the whole human race," she said as the beads sped through her fingers.

There was a pause to let that sink in. Twelve children gazed at each other and tried to guess what terrible mischief we had been up to. Spreading her hands in an evangelical posture, she went on. "Two thousand years ago Jesus died on the cross to redeem us and by this selfless act he made things better for us." There was a sigh of relief in the class.

The catechism was then learned off by heart, as the golden precepts of Catholicism were skilfully imparted. The bedrock of a belief that would last the rest of our lives. We would question it, and stray from it, but once a Catholic, always a Catholic, even if the return is at the eleventh hour.

Mary Horan marshalled us for our First Confession one Saturday morning. I was quite worried about the fact that I had eaten an apple knowing it to be stolen. The old priest did not seem to be terribly worried about it and I left the confessional with a great sense of relief.

On Sunday Mary Horan shepherded us to the altar rails to receive Holy Communion. I recall the rejoicing, the new clothes and the shiny half crowns from assembled relatives. At midday there was a lovely meal in the village hall. There was an ample supply of drinks for the parents and the day ended with a sing song and most of us had to give our party piece.

It leaves a lovely memory, the buzz of conversation and a lovely sense of community. We were not classified as infants any longer. The three R's took on a new importance and life took on a great seriousness. Very shortly now I would be wearing my first long trousers.

The time seemed to fly and one morning I found myself in senior school. This was different; there was a large blackboard with a cane in a prominent position and maps of the world all over the walls. There was a brief induction from a grim, forbidding, austere little man. Master Tom was a disciplinarian, with a strutting walk like a bantam cock.

"You will be with me for some time and I will endeavour to set you on the right road."

Looking back now I think he was a lonely man with a great love of learning. Deep down he knew that none of us would have the benefit of third level education. He did his best and stretched us to our limits. He could be severe and sarcastic but I suppose he had a lot to contend with.

My schooling finished on my fourteenth birthday. I feel I was reasonably prepared for life when I left. Further education would have been nice but economic reasons decreed otherwise.

The little schoolhouse is still standing, transformed into four luxury flats with sea views. I wonder if the new inhabitants ever think of past pupils scattered all over the world. The trees close by are much bigger now, but the tiny waterfall at the back still tinkles over the shiny stones. The stream close by looks the same as when we used its clear water to mix the ink and fill the ink wells for the classroom; a job always given to the most trustworthy of the pupils. Just a little imagination and on a still morning you can almost hear the unmistakeable voices of children at play.

CHILDHOOD MEMORIES

I cannot remember a downside; the sky was always blue, and when the sun glinted on the water I imagined that our harbour was awash with diamonds. Little boats rocked with a rhythm all of their own and I felt that the bridge that crossed the harbour was the biggest in the world.

Everything looks huge when you are a metre tall. Even now I have to remind myself that we also had storms and rainy days. It was great to stand barefoot in the rock pools and watch the waves breaking on the shore in a swirl of foam. When they receded they made sounds almost impossible to imitate. The nearest I can get to it is the slurping sounds my uncle made when he drank tea from a basin without his false teeth. It was their own music, endlessly polishing the pebbles on the beach.

Storms came at night. Howling Atlantic gales that rattled the slates on our roof and driving rain that lashed the window panes. Wrapped in my blankets I always felt safe and loved, and in my childish fantasies, I was on the deck of a sailing ship with the wind whistling through the rigging. Forked lighting occasionally lit up the walls of my bedroom. On those nights, my mother usually made the rounds of the house scattering holy water everywhere and praying fervently for all seafarers.

Warm and reassured, I never had a problem drifting back to sleep. When morning came the wild winds seemed to die down. The harbour was always a porridge colour, and necklaces of seaweed that had been torn from the rocks were strewn about everywhere.

I knelt on the window sill and watched the freighters wallowing by in the Atlantic swell. I always felt that the sea was a little sulky on those mornings as if disappointed that it had not caused more damage during the night. The funnels of the cargo boats always belched black smoke. I seemed to identify more with them than the occasional sleek liner that showed up on the horizon. Floating hotels, shaped like match boxes and catering to the caste system of the time.

With a mind like blotting paper and approaching seven, I began to realise that there was a great big world outside of our village. I heard seamen speak of foreign places with musical names like Valparaiso. Cities, with buildings, that almost reached the sky and rivers where men panned for gold.

My parents told me that I had relatives in New York, Sydney and London. They also told me that it was highly improbable that I would see them due to distance and cost. People lived and died in those times without ever being twenty miles from where they were born.

I was taken to one American wake. A great gathering of neighbours said goodbye to the emigrant, and in most cases they would never see him again. I was saddened by the tears, the music and the goodbyes. The next day we could see the liner that took the emigrant westwards. Bonfires were sometimes lit on the hills to be observed by the emigrant from the deck of the liner. The handshakes and hugs were over; from now on it would be the visit of the postman and the hope of some American dollars.

Despite one younger sister and a brother, I was a loner, it was the age of innocence and I could wander freely through the countryside. Fear of being accosted was unheard of and people often left their doors unlocked. Travellers and strangers were welcomed with open arms and offered food and drink. This in spite of people having very little themselves.

Green fields, dusty un-metalled roads, sheltered woodland dells awash with bluebells in season, and fences completely carpeted with primroses. Then there were the fuchsia hedges covered with red pendulous flowers and the hum of bees as they sucked nectar from their depths. I loved to imitate the bees sounds and suck some of the nectar myself, a never to be forgotten taste in that fairyland of noise and colour.

A daily journey for me would be to the head of the pier, with its unforgettable smells: salt water, fish, tar, hot oil, and the unmistakeable whiff of diesel over all. Each trawler with a rope from its bow wrapped around a bollard, and the whirr of the derricks as they hoisted out boxes of gleaming fish from the holds. The silver coloured harvest of the sea loaded onto lorries and despatched to places where I had never been. I was seven. I was fascinated; I wanted to be part of this, it would have been heaven to take the wheel on those boats and feel the thump of the diesel engine under my feet. I imagined the lift of her bow meeting the Atlantic swell as we sailed out against the sky. Why was it not possible to grow to manhood overnight?

In today's climate of laws, regulations and risk assessments, I would have been hunted off the pier, but then a little boy in short trousers I was allowed to stand and stare. It was a different age; a shout from an adult would have let me know if I was in danger or making a nuisance of myself.

One never to be forgotten day, I was invited by a kindly skipper to visit the wheelhouse on the *Atlantic Star*. I stood on a fish box and grabbed the spoked wheel. For a brief moment I felt I was one of the bronzed crew members. They gave me hot sweet tea in a white enamel mug. I listened to tales of storms, shipwrecks and strange happenings. The skipper told me "Never forget son, that a friend at sea is worth two on the land."

As I proudly stepped ashore afterwards I really felt, that I had been let in to one of life's great secrets.

Whilst in the tub that night, I told my mother of that day's great adventure. She had in fact guessed something about the days exploits; you cannot disguise the smell of fish, diesel and hot oil.

I was now attending infant's school. I made my own way as my sister and brother were taking up a lot of my mother's time. I could have gone by road but I much preferred to walk through the fields. There seemed to be a heavy dew on the grass before the sun came up, I took off my shoes and socks and it was sheer bliss to walk through the big meadow. There was that sensuous feel and I always thought it made my feet extra clean.

Before entering school I had to replace my shoes and socks. I always made sure to have an extra handkerchief for drying between my toes. Teacher was fussy about footwear.

"We are not an inner city school; we can all afford shoes here."

I suppose, "Just about," would have been the answer to that.

I never became close to the teacher; I never tried very hard. The sound of a ship's siren or the hum of a threshing machine made me lose interest in what he was trying to impart. Always longing for the three o'clock bell when I could dash away and see which trawler had docked, or see if there was a threshing in progress. Then, of course, there was the ploughing.

Two big horses drawing a plough, the sound it made as the blade cut in to the green sward. The screaming of excited sea gulls as they dived and swooped. Heaven knows what they did to the natural balance of things as they gobbled up earth worms as if there was no tomorrow.

It was all more exciting than school, but sadly after a while I had to conform. I had to knuckle down especially after a conversation in our parlour between the teacher and my parents. I tried to listen but they spoke in very low tones and their faces were serious when they emerged from the parlour. Who can resist the pressure from teachers, parents and priests?

Sadly the growing up process had started.

UNCLE JACK

The brown tinge at the ends of his moustache intrigued me. The rest of his moustache and indeed his unkempt hair was a silvery grey. With all the logic of an eight year old boy, I formed the opinion that the brown edges were caused by being immersed in Guinness frequently. He always addressed me as 'boy', and I grew quite close to him over the years.

He was tall with a spare gaunt frame, and had hollow cheeks that were always sunburned. My eyes were always drawn to his hands as he grasped oars or nets on his old yawl; they were callused and always seemed to have a black ring of dirt around his nails. Occasionally, he attempted to clean them. He used the same knife that he cut his tobacco with. It was never a successful manicure and always set my teeth on edge.

To the despair of my parents I tried to imitate some of his antics. They forbade me to wear one of his greasy old caps; I thought it made me look older but my mother insisted I wash my hair more often. Jack, being her brother, she had to be tactful. My mother, always clean, and the house spotless, was often mortified by Jack's cavalier attitude to household chores.

I can still picture him sitting in the stern of his decrepit old yawl, the old man of the sea, collarless shirt, frieze trousers, ragged old cap, and waistcoat shiny from probing hands, reaching for his tobacco plug. Then there was his excitement during the mackerel season.

"Look at them boy, watch them schooling; they go mad, look, they almost chase the sprats on to the rocks. Hardly need the nets boy; you could catch them in a bucket."

On the surface it felt as if I could walk on the thick shoals and reach the shore. Uncle Jack's eyes would be twinkling at this stage and he would always mutter, "God is good." Lots of fish meant lots of Guinness, interspersed with numerous glasses of whiskey, the yawl always tied up at the jetty as Jack and his mates worshipped Bacchus.

Jack paid six shillings a week for a four roomed cottage. It had a flag stoned floor, whitewashed walls and a slate roof. It was also built in a very exposed position and was always subject to the Atlantic gales.

"Would ye listen to that boy, that's coming all the way from America." The roof slates rattled and groaned on bad nights, but Uncle Jack wrapped in his blankets, and mostly anesthetised with the wine of our great nation, slept on.

Mornings were a re-birth and certain rituals were observed. I never saw him use a comb, just five fingers pushed through his hair. The ablutions were basic, just a dab of water on his face and the sleep rubbed from his eyes with the back of his hand. Next came a visit to the well for a galvanised bucket of sparkling water. Coming back he went on his knees, not to pray, but to wrestle with green timber and wet peat in an attempt to get a fire going. After a lot of effort, a small blaze used to glow in the hearth. Then it was time to start with the fire machine, as it was called. This was a bellows. Made by Pierce of Wexford, it was made of a cast iron body encasing a shaft with fixed vanes. This was connected by means of a leather drive belt to an eighteen inch diameter wheel. The air entered the underside of the fire by means of a duct that ran underneath the floor. There was a down side to the operation. Often when Jack was agitated, grasping the handle, he twisted it furiously. Showers of soot sparks and ashes went everywhere. Often I asked him to slow down but his answer was always the same.

"Don't worry about the dust boy, it takes a ton of dirt to kill you, and my carpets are fire proof."

He made porridge in a large black pot and usually enough to last him for a week. Sometimes he boiled a couple of eggs, and my mother always made sure he had a supply of freshly baked soda bread. All his meals were followed by a basin full of strong tea; he did not use cups. Asking my mother why he did not have best china like her, she'd say it was probably because he didn't have visitors. Breakfast over, he began to cut slices from a tobacco plug. Kneading it in his strong hands, he rammed it into the bowl of his turned down pipe. Picking up a glowing ember from the fire he set it alight. When pulling satisfactorily he set forth.

A dedicated beachcomber, he patrolled the harbour coastline every morning. I used to trot behind him on school holidays. There was always a collection of net buoys, glass bottles, and sometimes some useful timber. There was that memorable morning when he found a keg of brandy. I was sworn to secrecy. Rushing back to the jetty he jumped in his yawl, cast off and rowed as if he was in the sculls at Henley. I watched from the shore as he lassoed it and pulled it into the yawl. Covering it with an old sail he informed me that he was cancelling our fishing trip. A local publican was quick to convert the brandy into money, and conveniently forgot to inform Customs and Excise. In Uncle's case it meant many nights of great celebration, music and craic. My father commented one evening on seeing him coming from the pub.

"My God, you could light a forty watt bulb off his nose."

My mother resting after doing the weekly wash remarked, "Shure it's a blessing from God that he doesn't have money all the time, because if he had he would be a raving alcoholic."

Life is relentless. One miserable morning, Uncle found himself with trembling hands, a hacking cough and empty pockets. When I called to see him there were two empty Guinness bottles and a half bottle of whiskey on the table. I tried to get him to tell me about fishing during World War II. His heart wasn't in it. The blue eyes were bloodshot and had lost their twinkle. His face was grim and not improved by a two day growth of beard.

"What is the matter Uncle Jack?"

"Not a lot boy, I just spent my money fast and free with tales of the land and songs of the sea," he said with a sigh.

He had not bothered to light the fire that morning. We had not been out in his yawl for three weeks, and I knew contraband brandy had played a part in the way he put his hands on the table to stop them trembling.

"Uncle Jack why are you always thirsty?"

The roguish old face lit up a bit for the first time that morning. "It had to do with my baptism boy. The priest was old they tell me, his hand shook. When he put the salt on my tongue he must have overdone it. I have supped enough to float the Titanic since then, but it's never enough. I will tell you something boy, one drink is enough, two is too much, but then three isn't half enough." I suppose as a drunkard's philosophy, it has its place.

I knew he was at low ebb, and in a childish way I suppose I tried to offer some advice. I can remember his honest self-assessment when I told him to pull himself together and try to get a job.

"I have trained for nothing boy, and I was at the end of the queue when they gave out brains." It hurt to see him so demoralised.

"Uncle Jack, what about getting an outboard motor for the yawl?"

His answer was a classic. "Listen boy, the yawl is old and she hangs together by the grace of God; an outboard motor would shake her to bits, and we would both find a watery grave one evening. Not that I would mind for myself, but you have your life ahead of you. And another thing I am not mechanically minded."

Discussion from there in would have been sterile. Any capital outlay would have meant less money for drink. Banks, post offices and saving accounts did not rank very high in Uncle's scheme of things. Once I asked him if he ever thought about saving for his old age. He took me seriously.

"I have twenty pounds sewn into the lining of this cap. I am old so that's not a worry but that is for my burial. You are the only one that knows."

"You know you could live for another thirty years and that would not be enough."

"It will have to do boy, no one is left over the ground." Taking a long swig from a pint glass he said, "If they don't bury me for love they will have to because of stink." I can recall the shock, as Irishmen take wakes and funerals very seriously.

As for Jack himself, he attended all funerals. I can still smell the camphor balls when the one and only blue suit was taken from the cupboard. He prepared carefully and he once told me, "You must boy, it shows respect."

A strap for sharpening his cut throat razor hung from the back of the kitchen door and a little bit above it was a cracked, fly speckled mirror. The razor sang as he sharpened it and he lathered his face with the same soap he used to occasionally wash his clothes with. With cheeks glowing, highly polished black shoes and a navy polo-necked jersey he was ready to honour the dead.

The blue serge suits and that rig out were much favoured by fishermen of the time. During that era whiskey was freely given out in all graveyards and custom decreed that all available was consumed. In fact it was considered bad luck to take full bottles from the graveyard. When the rituals were complete most of the mourners adjourned to the local pubs. The deceased was praised and prayed for and toasts were drunk to his memory and his good deeds. You never spoke ill of the dead and Uncle Jack heartily approved of this lovely old custom. After funerals he usually floated home about midnight. If questioned about the funeral next day, he had a stock answer, "We gave him a proper send off."

I knew him in his middle years. He was the oldest of a family of five; he was ten years older than my mother and they were the only four to survive their infancy. His father died when he was thirteen. A country in turmoil, no state aid, a widowed mother and a younger brother to look after, he got a berth on a trawler at half a man's wage, which must have made a difference to the household.

This was about 1916. He seldom spoke of those years. Yeats said after the Irish rebellion and executions that a new and terrible beauty was born. I often wondered what effect it had on a teenager. About that time, I heard from a saloon bar patriot that it was better to die on your feet than live on your knees.

Watching him mend an old net in the stern of his yawl, I felt I should quiz him on this period of his life. "Uncle Jack why is it you never got involved?"

He looked up sharply. "You have been talking to Clancy. Listen boy, some of us are still on our knees and when you get older you will learn a lot more. My advice to you is, learn how to add up and read and write. Leave politics to those who can shoot around corners."

I never quite understood the last bit. Jack's career as a trawler man was brought to an abrupt end at the outbreak of the Second World War, when along with half a dozen others he was sunk by a German U boat. The fish they caught was being sold in England and the Fuhrer wanted to starve the Brits. Uncle Jack was now unemployed. In the interim years his mother had died and he had married and lost his young wife in child birth.

Compensation from Lloyds was a cheque for £100. This would have been for the loss of personal effects. He told me that in his haste when the U boat skipper told them to get in the punt before hitting their boat below the water line, he left a pair of leaky wellingtons and a torn oilskin aboard. The filling of their claim form was carried out by someone with a vivid imagination. A local publican cashed the cheque, and it was the beginning of Jack's heavy drinking.

"It was the most money I had seen in my life boy, I thought it would never end." It was not the beginning of a great financial empire or indeed any kind of success.

By the end of the forties things began to get a little better. Jack swallowed the anchor and got a job with the local council. Despite his mechanical ineptitude he finished up driving a steam roller. Highly delighted with a steady income, he measured his wages in pints and small whiskeys.

Giving me his yawl, he vowed never to leave dry land again. Occasionally my mind goes back to evenings spent with him in that boat. I can almost hear the slap of the waves against the keel. Twilights were magic - a calm evening, the sun sinking slowly in the west and the shadows chasing each other over the water, as if they were trying to catch the sun before it disappeared. Then, just before dark, the raucous noise of the homeward bound rooks; they nested in the wood across the harbour. Uncle Jack, pipe well alight, the old man of the sea sitting in the stern, looking up at the returning birds. "Would ye look at them boy, blotting out the sky. De Valera's air force."

COUSIN MIKE

Our village consisted of seventy-four people, and Cousin Mike hated every one of them. He was a fat little man with a tonsure and a red face that went a puce colour when he was angry. These outbursts happened frequently and the cotton wool like hair that ballooned over his ears seemed to stand out rigidly on these occasions.

Aged about nine at the time, I was the only one he allowed past his front door. As evening shadows fell he stood on a chair near a window and observed the happenings of the village. When all the oil lamps in the village were lighting he used to mutter. “The slums are lighting now boy.” He would then commence to fill and light his own lamp. Paraffin was poured from a can he kept under the table and the globe was cleaned with a page from the *Western Star*. His hands shook, but spillages were ignored, and anyhow, the smell of paraffin is not unpleasant.

This ritual never altered; no doubt he had his own reasons for waiting for the rest of the villagers. I remember how nice it was to sit and smell the smoke from his open peat fire. The shadows from the fire would dance on the blue ware on his dresser. These were from his mother’s time, never used now and were covered with a thick layer of dust.

He had continuous trouble and bitter feuds with all his neighbours. Local police knew him well and all his latest antics were reported at the village pump. Bishops, priests and the local justice of the peace had him on their files, and my parents, for sure, were not happy with my friendship with this cantankerous old man. Often at meal times mother used to say, “I wish you would keep away from that man, he doesn’t go to mass, church or meeting and even the priest says that he is quite disturbed."

My father took a more relaxed attitude. "I shouldn't worry about it, it's only a matter of time until you are off his mailing list and he will bar you from the house eventually."

It never happened. I listened to his wild diatribes, his ranting and raving about imagined insults and wondered about what was going on in his head. Reasoning with him was not an option and I think he used me as a kind of a wailing wall.

For my part I think I learned what had made him so bitter. It was a wet evening and he was having difficulty with wet peat and a fire that was smoking badly. Things like this often brought on rages.

"Did you hear from America at Christmas?"

"Not for years now boy, they are all doing well in Boston, but never think of Mike. When the mother and father died I looked after them. Fed and clothed them and when they were hardy sent them to my eldest sister in America. Fishing was good at the time and when it went bad I got somebody to write to my sister, I hoped she would sponsor me in the States." Getting very agitated at this stage he furiously turned the handle of the fire machine and coated the place in another layer of dust and ashes.

"Let me show you boy." Standing on a chair he took down a Fox's Glacier Mints box from the clevvy and handed me a letter. "Read what it says boy, from my own sister."

The beginning dealt with all the family gossip of his tribe but the final lines are carved on my memory. *"Mike, I feel that America is not for you, as I think we have plenty like you here already."* I folded the letter and put it back in the box.

Returning it to the clevvy, he muttered, "Eaten bread is soon forgotten boy."

I knew that at that period he had been a heavy drinker but I am glad his sister was not in the diplomatic service. That must have been the time when the iron entered into his soul. His emotions boiled over and ever afterwards he was at war with the world. His faith in human nature never recovered.

Now unemployed, his assets were a four roomed cottage, a donkey and cart, and one acre of fertile land. He commenced to grow vegetables for the Dublin market. This came as a great surprise to most of his neighbours and they put it down to another of his little oddities. I think it might have had a calming effect on this cantankerous, tortured man. He carefully laid out beds and manured them with seaweed from the local strand. Early potatoes were his main crops but he also dabbled in carrots and parsnips

His south facing garden became a place of beauty and was even mentioned in one of the periodicals of the time. His rough callused hands picked and carefully packed the early produce in boxes. The boxes were then sent by rail to the Dublin market. Having a feud with the local Station Master, this meant he had to tackle his donkey and cart to take his packages to the next village. I frequently helped him during gluts, at weekends and after school.

Because of his illiteracy, another of my jobs was to write letters to auctioneers in the Dublin markets. Standing in front of the fire, he dictated and I had to filter out the vile and abusive language. Most of the communications had to do with bad prices for his products; unfortunately, he never grasped the connection between oversupply and falling prices. Eventually, under his guidance I contacted the Ministry of Agriculture and Fisheries about the raw deal that the West of Ireland growers were getting for their produce. A beautifully crafted letter was received in reply. Listening carefully while I read the reply, his face went a puce colour and leaping to his feet he began to pace the floor.

"Fuck him!" he said banging the table. "Hanging is too good for that hoor; it's a kick in the bollocks he wants." I still cannot work out any logic in that statement.

The upshot was that I had to send another missive to the Department. Doubts were cast on the minister's parentage and fucks were more plentiful than reasoned argument. It was not a very long letter when edited, and I guess it is gathering dust in some government archive still.

There was a general election held shortly afterwards. Elections are taken very seriously in our village and politicians are never sure of your vote unless they visit you personally and listen to your concerns. They usually know their supporters, so that cuts out some of the leg work. Mike was probably to the left and during that election I have memories of a little red-faced man being chased from his door. Clutching his manifestoes, he had just asked for his vote; instead he was chased by a lunatic grasping a two prong pike.

Contacts with government had reinforced his view that they were all a pack of stealing bastards who were robbing him blind. Living hand to mouth, he kept his head above water by sheer hard work.

One of his most onerous tasks was to collect seaweed for fertiliser. Loading this on to his donkey cart he hauled it to his garden and spread it on the beds before planting. It was free but laborious. Previous to this he had to tackle the donkey. This was always achieved with difficulty. The donkey's first owner had treated him badly and for ever more left him with a suspicious nature. Mike tied ropes out of him everywhere whilst he attempted to put on his harness, collar, straddle and winkers. This operation was usually carried out with Mike pouring out a litany of vile curses on his previous owners and all their relations. Occasionally, even when tackled, the donkey lashed out and beat a tattoo on the rickety old cart.

One day at the start of the operation, in all the confusion, the ropes got twisted around Mike's legs. The donkey took flight and dragged him through a fuchsia hedge and into his neighbour's field. Badly shook up after this episode, he sold him to the travellers and for some strange reason bought a jennet. Jennets are ungainly animals at the best of times and with his horse's head and donkey's body this one was no exception. Supposedly stronger than a donkey, they have teeth like a camel and this particular one always had his tongue hanging out.

A tall imperious looking lady called Mrs Clert had settled in our village. In her youth, it was reported that this lady had spent a lot of her time shouting at native servants in India.

Probably to make up for that she was now very interested in animal welfare. Spotting Mike and his jennet one day she addressed him. "My good man, why does your animal have his tongue hanging out?"

"Just to let air to his arse Mrs," he said.

She tapped her silver-headed walking cane angrily and walked on. This was no way for a peasant to speak to his betters. She joined a long list of people who no longer spoke to him.

Unfortunately, his paranoia increased as the years rolled on. He became more and more isolated and his feverish imagination ran riot. He no longer visited pubs as they were intent on poisoning him. Neighbours were stealing his peat and vegetables. During the hours of darkness his roof was constantly bombarded with showers of stones and occasionally the crack of rifle fire. People were constantly slandering him, listening at his door and criticising his mode of dress. The police were called frequently and he now visited the doctor's private residence because to add to his problems he had become a raving hypochondriac. Feeling that he had every disease, he stuffed cupboards full of potions and bottles. I laughed at his imaginary complaints, and he called me a callous little bastard, but I was still the only one he left past his front door.

I relayed all messages from local officialdom, waited for the storm of bad language to die down and then tried to sort out some of his aggravations. The local doctor was quite concerned and asked me frequently about his welfare. Social Services were thin on the ground in the forties; I probably was the only link.

One evening when I delivered some groceries I noticed a change. I told my parents that his speech was slurred and he had not been drinking. Events moved quickly and an ambulance was called. Somehow the elders took over then and I was pushed into the background. He was taken straight to hospital and died shortly afterwards.

I fed his jennet that night, my face awash with tears. Somehow I think I had pierced the barrier he had erected between himself and the rest of the human race, even to the fact that he had once told me that he wished to be buried with his mother.

To everyone's surprise he had made a will and left his house and a small sum of money to his nephew who was a bishop in America. It was a big surprise because when this church man had attempted to visit him a few years previously he had slammed the door in his face. I was entrusted with the care of his jennet. Luckily, a kindly gentleman from the next parish took him off my hands rather quickly.

His cottage is now a six bedroomed bungalow with a beautifully landscaped garden. I visit his grave whenever I can. I can still picture him quite clearly. I hope he found peace in the next life as he had very little in this.

AUNT MARGRETH

Aunt Margreth walked with a limp. This was due to having no heel on her left leg. As a child I learned that this was due to having it shot off. As a young woman she had clashed with the forces of occupation. I cannot remember being angry about this but I was always inquisitive and would have loved to have seen it.

Wearing long black dresses and with her grey hair drawn in to a severe bun, I wondered at the steel knitting needle that was always stuck in it. Seldom going out, except to do some shopping, her one social outing was to church on Sunday, always in the same pew and at a distance from others.

Her neighbours kept her in their sights and always had a tale to tell about the comings and goings at her house. These visitations were usually at night, mostly men, and all with the grey pallor of people who had not led an outdoor life for some time.

Lots of the younger generation called her 'Miss' but she did have a husband. They had married in the local church. During the wedding reception he had left through a door at the back of the hall and was not seen for the next twenty-five years. It was unusual and the reasons were always discussed in low whispers. Later it was known that he became a first mate on a ship in the great lakes in America. Unlike a lot of his shipmates he had lived aboard and accumulated quite a lot of money. My Uncle Jack witnessed his home-coming and he doubted very much that his wife knew he was arriving. Stepping off the late night bus complete with a seaman's kit bag he rapped politely on her door. Admitting him without warmth or welcome she did however insist on seeing his bank book. Uncle Jack said that it must have been satisfactory as she ushered him to his own bedroom.

It would seem that they lived happily from there on in. As an adult I asked my uncle if he felt the marriage had ever been consummated. His answer was short and sweet: "How the fuck do I know?" I pursued it no further.

In the mid-forties Margreth got a living as a dressmaker. Her customers were of a certain age. Fashion changes would have been completely ignored and I suppose her charges reflected the lack of haute couture. Occasionally I was asked to drop off some material at her house. I did not enjoy those visits. I can remember the whirr of the foot pedal operated Singer sewing machine and the way the leaves on a calendar that hung near her open door used to flap and rustle. Conversations with her took on the order of an interrogation.

"Can you speak our language? Are you being taught Irish history at school? Not the revised and watered down version, I hope?"

Sometimes she rearranged my fringe, with fingers showing signs of arthritis, and scratched her back with one of her long knitting needles.

"You must never forget that we have four green fields and one of them is still planted." Her eyes flashed when she said that and I could detect a sort of foam at the corners of her mouth. It was just like the surf that you see at the edge of breakers as they fall on the strand.

Somewhere there is a faded photograph of a boy of seven, short trousers, laced up black shoes, socks folded back below the knee, and an unruly head of curls. Margreth took that on the day my brother Bill was born. The camera, a gift from her brother who was a high ranking army officer.

Bill, like the rest of us, was born in the bed he was conceived in. I was sent to Margreth's that day. It would not have been my parent's first choice but I think events caught up with them. They had seen the horrors of civil war and now they just wanted peace and a good life for their children. Deep down they thought that this unreformed rebel might influence a wax like mind. That morning, the district nurse, riding a bike with high handle bars had arrived. I know I was confused and frightened. In that age the mysteries of birth and procreation were not explained to the young. I am certain that having a child under her care for a day would have been a trial to Auntie.

"What would you like to do Patrick?"

"Can we play snakes and ladders?"

"I do not have a board or dice. Let me tell you some of the stories of our nation."

All morning she read of Cuchullain, Setanta, the Hill of Tara, and the ancient High Kings. When she got to the Battle of Kinsale her voice broke and her face took on a great sadness. My eyes must have been glazed by then because she jumped up and closed the book.

"I think we should have some lunch. Is chicken OK?"

"That will be lovely, Aunt Margreth."

"Well, follow me then."

Taking a sharp knife from the dresser she walked ahead of me to the yard. Moving stealthily amongst a flock of chickens, she grabbed a squawking victim. Grasping it between her legs, she stretched its neck and drew the razor-sharp knife across it. It shuddered for some time with blood dripping onto the dusty yard. The rest of the flock looked on inquisitively and I felt a band of icy terror across my stomach.

Feeling sick, I watched her pluck and prepare the chicken. Stopping for a moment, she looked at me. "Are you feeling alright?"

"Did the chicken suffer?"

"Of course not, and let's have no more of that silliness from you. The Lord gave us dominion over the fowls of the air and all the animals on earth."

As people do, I shuttered the incident in my mind and, to my shame, never became a vegetarian.

A myth sometimes grows up about people like my aunt. My parents were always a little hesitant in their dealings with her and when I asked questions they steered the conversation in another direction. Parents are quite naive on what children pick up on.

I can still see the profusion of geraniums in her living room and the sleek well fed blind cat that had adopted her. I am convinced that he resented visitors. Travelling people called often and never left without a little food or money. During an outbreak of robberies in our village, she was never once troubled. I mentioned this strange fact to my Uncle Jack, who just said, “The toe rags know better.”

Watching him draw deeply on his pipe, at nine, I could not fully understand the undercurrents that ran deeply in our troubled history.

I never did get to see her heel. At twelve, I had lost a lot of my childish fears and decided to ask her. “Auntie, does your heel pain you at times?”

“Who told you about my heel?”

“Well, I thought everyone knew.”

“It was before your time child, we had to rely on treatment in safe houses. The pain and risk of poor treatment was preferable to being shot or imprisoned. We were thin on the ground and my cousin was in the prison camp in Wales.” She began to pace the floor clenching and un-clenching her hands. “Now the fat cats in Dublin have decided to give us a pension of seven and six a week, we the people who made their superannuated jobs possible. I see them drive past some days, chauffer driven cars and Ulster crombies, gombeen men the lot of them, men who have never heard the rattle of a machine gun or spent a night on a wet hillside.”

Quite agitated by now she tried to make tea with cold water. “It’s a funny old life Patrick, but we must try to keep the faith, as we have never been short of saloon bar patriots.” I thought I saw a tear in the corner of her eye.

My parents were serious and silent when I told them of our conversation. Without forbidding me to spend time with Margreth I picked up the atmosphere. They did not approve.

Margreth outlived her husband and because of his money was quite comfortable in her later years. Money did not affect her lifestyle but Uncle Jack did tell me that she had an unending supply of financial wizards telling her how to manage her new found wealth. Nothing changes.

I went to her funeral in the mid-eighties. Wind blew in from the Atlantic that day and the rain bucketed down. The mourners were few as she had outlived most of the old brigade - there was barely a dozen, and yet there were four priests. Wood pigeons kept up a chorus during the service and the surrounding trees rustled and shook in the autumn wind. As the coffin was being lowered into the ground, two men complete with black berets and gloves, stepped from behind the trees, pointing revolvers to the sky, and they fired a last salute.

Wood pigeons departed en masse, and the priest's recitations of graveside prayers never faltered. Knowing glances were exchanged as the men stepped back into the trees. There were some who shook my hand. I know I shed a tear. It was the end of an era and the shouts of school children, playing in the distance, seemed to give the whole thing some meaning.

I refused a lift from the graveyard; I needed some time on my own, and to spend some time in the old church. I know I prayed for the soul of this strange old aunt of mine, buried in the old windswept hill overlooking the Atlantic.

Her will could only be speculated about by the gossips. There was never a headstone erected and yet her husband, buried in another graveyard, had a very ornate headstone. A lot of priests at her funeral led people to believe that the church had benefitted. My gut feeling is that another organisation got her money. God alone knows; may the sod rest lightly on her.

WASH DAY

"Cleanliness is next to Godliness," she used to say. Every Monday morning, in fine weather mother put that into practice.

"You must have a method," she used to say, and she certainly planned wash day like a military exercise.

At seven in the morning I stoked up the range, and stacked dry logs and peat close by. Before going to school I made sure to bring six buckets of water from the well, which was a couple of hundred yards away.

I always got a special hug before leaving for school.

"Aw shure you have given me a great start to the day, alannah." She still had to haul countless buckets of water during the day, and despite being small and petite, she was no stranger to hard physical work.

The ritual never varied. All the rings on the hob were occupied by pots of boiling water. The huge galvanised oval shaped bath was placed on the table, the washing board also placed within easy reach. Sheets were stripped from the beds, put in the tub and sprinkled with Rinso. Pots of boiling water poured onto the clothes and always replenishing the supply. All this was carried out whilst she topped and tailed, as she put it, my younger siblings.

Rubbing the clothes on the wash board, dunking them back in to the hot sudsy water and then squeezing the water from them before dunking them in a bucket of cold water, another squeeze and with a final flap hanging them on the line. She did not believe in and had no use for a mangle. Discussing the technology one day with my aunt, she said, "It's no good; it wrinkles the clothes and makes the ironing hard work."

Our clothes line was strung across the garden and anchored to an ash tree at each side. When it was fully loaded she placed a prop in the centre, which stopped sheets dragging on the ground and took some of the strain.

On breezy days it came alive, and with the sheets billowing and flapping they gave off a noise like the rigging on a sailing ship. After school I often helped her bring in the dry washing. Sometimes the washing wrapped itself around me, especially when it was very breezy. There is a very distinct smell from linen warmed by the sun and dried by ozone laden sea breezes.

Clothes pegs and their construction were the bane of my mother's life. At that time they were made of soft wood with a very inferior wire spring in the middle, they often snapped with disastrous results. It could mean her clean sheets ending up in our neighbour's ploughed field. This always entailed another session with the wash board. The wash board consisted of two straight pieces of wood, eighteen inches apart and connected by densely packed half inch round dowels. The suds and water ran through them and I suppose they were an improvement to bashing clothes on stones in the river. Two decades later they were used by musicians as skiffle boards.

My mother's clothes peg supplier was a gypsy woman called Maggie. She must have been psychic as she always rapped on our door when mother's clothes pegs were running low. A tall striking looking woman, her hair was drawn tightly against her face and finished up in a pigtail which reached her waist. Her face was a deep copper colour, her legs were slightly bandy and she always carried a large woven willow basket. No salesmanship required; their business was transacted in minutes. Mother always invited her in for tea and a slice of cake. Sitting at our kitchen table she took large slugs of the hot tea. There was always a slurping sound similar to a draw on the rocks, made by the ebb and flow of a tidal wave. Perspiring freely, a little mole on her chin seemed to shine. She slapped mother's best china on to the saucer. I always felt mother's tension fearing the loss of her best china.

I was intrigued by this woman. Most of the people I knew lived in our village and I felt there was an air of romance about this woman who travelled widely, so one day I struck up a conversation.

"Do you live close by, mam?"

Replacing her cup with a clatter on the saucer, she compressed her lips and her mouth took on the appearance of a rat clamp. "I have no fixed abode a gradh, Cromwell dispossessed my people. He drove us off our lands. 'To hell or to Connacht,' he said. May he burn and sizzle in hell for all eternity." With that she grabbed her basket and strode down our garden path as if she fully intended to stoke up the fires of hell.

Mother pursed her lips and looked at me. "You should not ask personal questions." Funny that, as dad had advised that I should always ask if I did not know.

For some strange reason, two cousins, Lyn and Ina, always arrived on wash day. They must have known that mother was busy, however, they parked their bicycles at our front door and were always received, courteously. They sat outside on fine days and mother supplied them with pots of tea and slices of fruit cake.

Cousin Lyn was stone deaf and her only interest was a feral cat called whiskey. She had an over active thyroid and could not stop talking, she never waited for an answer as she answered her own questions.

"We know you are busy Mary, Monday is your wash day, I know it is. Told Lyn so this morning, didn't I Lyn?" said Ina.

"Cats were worshipped in ancient Egypt they say, Ina," Lynn remarked to the air.

"She is getting worse you know can't hear a single word I say," Ina said to my mother.

Lyn just flicked crumbs from her black dress and stared in to the middle distance, both on their own wave lengths and completely happy in each other's company. Ina occasionally patted us children on the heads but did not approve of us as we sometimes interrupted her one sided conversations. They usually left when they saw mother getting ready for ironing. Apologising for arriving on her busy day they mounted their bicycles, and rode off at a sedate pace. The bicycles had no cross bar and they seemed to tidy their long dresses with care. Somehow, they never got entangled in the chain.

Often calling on me to keep the fire well stoked up, mother put two irons on the fire; these were triangular pieces of iron complete with handles. When one was hot it was put in what was called a slipper. This was a triangular piece of shiny plated steel and the hot iron fitted snugly in to it. Flicking some water at the surface to check that the heat was being conducted, mother began the lengthy process of ironing. A succession of irons had to be kept up as they cooled quickly and lost their efficiency. Dad's shirts got special attention, all had detached collars, and it was a mark of a good housewife how her husband looked .The collars attached by a stud were changed daily. I found it fascinating to watch. For hours it continued, the clunk of the iron, the hiss as the iron went over a damp patch. I fed peat to the fire and occasionally filled up a jug of water, this was for sprinkling on the linen. She sometimes sang to herself as she watched the pile of beautifully ironed linen grow. Long days, repetitive work, no electricity, and never a complaint. No television, and holidays unheard of.

Simple pleasures; her house clean, food on the table, and her family 'well turned out' as she called it.

CON CONNOR or CC

CC bore his enormous belly majestically through the little town of Carra. Six foot seven and weighing in at twenty two stone, his three chins wobbled as he plodded the pavements. Visiting his constituents he doffed his hat so frequently that shiny grease marks were visible on the brim.

Carra was his fiefdom and he represented it well in the big city. Known by all as CC, this could stand for his name or indeed County Councillor. Daily he tucked his great frame in to his little model T Ford and drove to the big city. A shiny ring on his waistcoat showed the rubbing of the steering wheel on his paunch. Herculean labours in the corridors of power were faithfully recorded in the local rag. The editor was an old school pal and drinking partner.

Some look on politics as the last resort of the scoundrel but CC was as genuine as you could find. He had drifted in to politics. His mother kept a pub much frequented by the movers and shakers of the town and it was here that he became interested. Brushing against polemics and dialectics at university he always took an active role in late night, alcohol inspired debates. Gaining credence with his listeners, they always seemed safe with his middle of the road philosophy.

Despite being a town dweller he was the farmer's candidate and always headed the poll at local elections. Holding his surgeries at the back of his mother's pub, no matter how minor the problem; he gave everyone his fullest attention. Hammering away at local issues and being quite formidable in debate, he had a fair success rate. Another advantage he had was that all his business was conducted at ground level, as he shied away completely from climbing stairs.

At first mass on Sundays he took up the collection. In his best black suit and his bald head shining in the candle light, the parishioners knew that he also had their spiritual needs at heart. The town did not have a Mayor but if we had CC would have filled that position with great decorum.

CC served his community well for fifteen long years and then came the moment when his political career should have moved to the higher echelons. Radio and newspapers brought news of the death of our local affairs minister. A by-election was triggered and a local candidate had to be selected. Informed opinion had it that CC should be the man. There was an air of great expectancy in the town. Much to our surprise he was opposed. Miss Hendry, a cultured woman of forty, with a first class degree in politics and economics, came on the scene. Newly widowed and with a young family, she made inroads in to CC's power base.

Her father had been in jail during the rebellion and that in itself was worth a lot of votes. Lobbying and horse trading went on apace for two weeks before the selection committee gave their decision. The town hall was crowded for the great announcement.

CC was not elected for high office and when he heard the announcement he seemed to shrink. Offering his congratulations, he slunk in to the night. His friends were surprised and called daily at his pub to commiserate.

His mother had died the previous month. Awash with sadness and disappointment, he began to drink very heavily. It now seemed that the heart had gone out of the man. Fair weather friends began to disappear and he was soon surrounded by hooks, crooks and broken down clergymen. His hat grew greasier and his hair, or what remained of it, grew unkempt. His three chins were no longer carefully shaved and his already red face was beginning to turn a deep purple. With mother dead, shirts were no longer carefully laundered and his waistcoat and tie were dotted with beer and food stains.

Somewhere in his whiskey fuddled brain he formed the opinion that the fact that he was unmarried, had barred him from high office. A circle of piss artists and hangers on did nothing to dispel this notion. His closest friend and confidant now was a vet called Henry Grattan. This gentleman spoke words of wisdom, and heartily endorsed marriage, despite the fact that he had avoided it like the plague.

CC became intrigued by the idea of matrimony. A wife would more than likely revive his flagging career because he knew he had still a lot to offer. Furthermore, he missed the care and attention his mother had provided. Despite being fifty three, Henry said, "You are in the prime of life, and the love of a good woman will not stunt your growth."

There seemed to be a surfeit of advice.

Teddy, a drunken old doctor struck off for an unhealthy interest in young boys, maintained that there were pitfalls. "CC has had neither a heterosexual or homosexual relationship up to now and it is my considered opinion that he is a Middlesex."

Liz Mac who was quite knowledgeable was heard to mutter, "God that must be an American thing; I never heard of one of those."

Jerry, a failed Dublin politician, had another point of view. "If CC gives himself the time, and lays off the booze, by keeping focussed, everything will be tickety boo."

Liz Mac chimed in again. "Of course the poor man will be OK, the old drink is a curse; increases desire and ruins performance they say."

About this time in Ireland the match making system was going out of fashion, and CC would have to start wooing or courting, as it was called. Up to that time a suitable young lady had not been mentioned. The local street cleaner had a widowed sister who had glanced sideways at CC a few times. However, he felt she was too small, and if truth be known, too far down the social scale.

A gin sodden retired teacher felt he should say a few words about her. "Size does not matter; if she finds it onerous to cock her slippers to the sky and risk getting smothered, she can always behave like a lustful lioness."

The street cleaner took umbrage at this. "We are a respectable family and the missionary position has stood us in good stead up to now, we will have none of your foreign perversions."

CC looked thoughtful, may be even a little lecherous. The teacher nodded off once more.

CC bought new clothes, changed his car for a bigger model and kept a diamond ring permanently in his waistcoat pocket. He also made it known that his late mother's earrings would adorn the lady of his choice. Liz Mac offered him a preview of marriage, "Just for the earrings love." He declined.

Mrs O'Riordan, his barmaid and housekeeper since his mother's death, was proposed to one night, when CC was in his cups. "Well thank you CC but I have a husband already, or I think I have somewhere in Australia."

Afterwards she said to another lady in the flower arranger's club, "He is having a midlife cirrhosis my dear."

Henry the vet, and his chief advisor was in America at the time and he had no real guidance in affairs of the heart.

After a few more attempts CC was beginning to panic, and put an advert in the matrimonial columns in *Ireland's Own.* He received just two replies. One came from a founder member of a divorced and desperate club inviting him to a grab a granny night at a local venue. Writing back in beautiful copperplate, he explained that he wanted a family and furthermore divorcees and separated were unacceptable as he had a political career to consider.

Miss Hayes, the second lady, arranged to meet him on neutral ground. They met at the Station Hotel on a wet Sunday afternoon. CC had been drinking steadily all morning. This refined, well brought up young lady looked at this huge blue faced man stinking of whiskey and Old Spice after shave. She politely, made her excuses and took the next train out of town.

Lothario sadly made his way back to his pub and his whiskey bottle. Telling the expectant throng of saloon bar lizards that he had just been through his darkest hour, he took to his bed for the rest of the day.

The darkest hour is before the dawn, even if it's a false dawn. Henry, our local vet and stud, had outlived his welcome in the US of A, resuming his practice, especially the part where he spent his evening in CC's Bar. With his waxed moustache and phoney American accent our Henry had reinvented himself.

The host told him the whole sad story of unsuccessful courtships and rejections. Henry listened with sympathy and asked for a little time to consider his predicament. "CC my friend, I will not desert you in your hour of need. We shall reconvene this meeting tomorrow at seven."

Liz Mac was heard to exclaim, "My God, would ye listen to him, he is full of bullshit and him not even a full blown Yank."

Seated on the high stool next evening, cigar glowing and a glass of Jameson in his right hand, Henry told CC of his efforts on his behalf. "You will know of the O' Dells, CC, they are the biggest pig breeders in the land. I have had professional dealing with the family for twenty years. Now, Nuala is prepared to go for a drive with you on Sunday."

CC did not look entirely happy. "She is past child bearing age, and rumour has it that she hates men."

Henry got off the high stool and placed his hands on CC's shoulders. "CC my friend, do you really want the bother of a family? There is a population explosion and surely you as a leader of men should show an example and discourage that sort of thing. And another thing, the dew of the morning is gone off yourself."

CC gave this a little consideration and muttered, "I suppose you are right."

Henry went on to say, "As to the second part of the problem, there is no such thing as a man hater. We will meet before Sunday and I will give you some guidance on that score."

Henry and CC met at local hotel on Saturday night. They chose a secluded corner. Discussing a delicate matter, they wanted to avoid ear flapping and gossip. The waiter said they consumed a bottle of whiskey, but still CC felt apprehensive as Henry gave his instructions.

"Valet the car, no drinking in the morning, have a bath and shave carefully and before you dress dab a little of this under your arms." He handed CC a bottle of colourless liquid. "Never mind what it is, it will give you confidence." They parted at midnight vowing eternal friendship.

Henry was remiss in not explaining about the mysterious potion. Pigs are notorious as lazy lovers and their courtship can sometimes take days. Sows, contrary to popular opinion are incredibly shy. Vets have been aware of this problem for decades. When a new product, called Boarmate came on the market it revolutionised everything. The industry immediately gave it the seal of approval. A little of this potion dabbed on the Boar made him irresistible and the whole performance was speeded up. Sows were ecstatic, boars took on a new lease of life and vets with this product were welcomed with open arms in all piggeries. Another side issue was of course that profits increased by leaps and bounds.

On Sunday morning CC's hands shook, but he knew he had to avoid the 'easy start'. Following his mentor's instructions to the letter, all went well until he went to dab on the potion. With his hands shaking like ivy leaves, the bottle slipped and he was drenched from head to foot. With no time for further washing, and in any case it seemed to smell of nothing to humans, at 11am CC sallied forth. Henry, with the great power of suggestion had done wonders for his confidence. The sun was shining and he began to feel optimistic. Things were on the up and up.

O'Dell's piggery was eight miles from the town, which was just as well as the smell was atrocious. Nuala and her brother John ran a very successful business and when the weather was fine they let their pigs run free. That morning, a thousand pigs ran free in their meadows and orchards, as CC parked his valeted car.

Nuala stood with her arms folded at the front door. A well preserved, pleasant woman in her late fifties, she watched CC heave and extricate his huge bulk from his car. She patted her iron grey hair, gave a last glance in the hall mirror and stepped out to welcome CC. Suddenly the whole world went mad. Half a dozen sows surrounded her date and began to nuzzle him. Four more feeling neglected decided to join in. Three younger sows feeling jealous led a charge and the great lover lost his footing and disappeared under a litter of lustful sows. Both his size twelve's were pulled from his feet and a disgruntled old boar trampled on his best hat. With his best suit and shirt in shreds, somehow he got to his feet and ran to climb a gnarled old apple tree. Covered in mud and almost stark naked his great quivering mass perched on the branches. The tree surrounded by squealing pigs, CC strove to cover his manhood as his testicles swung in the mid-morning breeze.

Nuala laughed so much her mascara ran and she retreated to the house for a bout of hysterics. Her brother hearing all the commotion ran to the front of the house. Quickly assessing the situation he tried to get the pigs behind closed doors.

"I bet they lose weight with all this excitement," he said to his sister, "and I never want to see that silly bastard within five miles of this place again". He kept glancing at the naked CC and warned his sister not to keep peeping through the window.

Calm eventually descended on this strange scene but John could not supply his unwanted guest with any clothes, he himself being a man of small stature and CC being a giant. Eventually wrapped in a huge coloured curtain CC drove back to his pub and took to his bed.

Two days later he reappeared, looking very subdued. He had made up his mind to remain a bachelor, as he felt his heart could not cope with all the stress and excitement. He never again sought female company and became very cool to Henry the vet.

Henry had tried to repair the damage. "Just a misunderstanding, old chap, you were meant to dab it not bloody marinade yourself in it."

He carried on his council duties with a new found enthusiasm after that. Well respected by all, he dropped dead on the golf course at eighty. His name in brass letters is now in the roll of honour in our town hall.

HENRY GRATTAN

Shop windows, book covers, and business cards never tell the whole story. Henry Grattan, our local vet, had just one business card. It was badly crumpled and the letters after his name were smudged. The highlights of his academic career would forever remain a mystery.

Never having had a shop window, he lodged with his three sisters in a large rambling farmhouse on the outskirts of the town. They addressed him as Mr Grattan and felt that he raised their standing amongst the social classes of the time. Despite using one of their rooms as an office, most of his consultations were carried out on the high stool in CC's bar. Born with a ferocious thirst, some of his diagnostic observations were rather wide of the mark.

He dressed like a member of the aristocracy. Bow tie, tweed hacking jacket, cavalry twill trousers and tweed cap were worn as his business uniform. He had long ago dispensed with his white coat and during difficult animal births he just acted in an advisory capacity. A glass of whiskey clutched in his right hand and a cigar glowing in his left, he read *The Times* between nine and ten each morning. This ritual complete, he set forth to minister to all sick animals and reassure their owners.

Home visits were a bit of a challenge. His Ford was big and shiny but terribly ancient. Despite the lack of traffic in the early forties, it also had a series of dents and scratches. Heavy drinking never improves driving and local farmers with tractors frequently had to rescue him from disasters.

His sisters Maggie, Helen, and Ina defended him vehemently when he was accused of drunkenness.

"He is always tired, the poor man, driving all those miles and not getting paid sometimes; the man is a walking saint. We are so lucky to have Dr Grattan."

Henry loved their loyalty and always referred to them as his ladies. With oodles of charisma he was indeed a ladies' man. Henry lodging with his sisters, probably was the reason why he never married. He fathered four children with four different women in the parish. He must have suffered from amnesia as he denied fatherhood in each case. When the ladies took him to court for breach of promise and failing to contribute, he pleaded loss of memory in each case. One judge noted that he must be the most forgetful man in Ireland, but said that in mitigation alcohol was contributing to his lapses. His sisters said that women were taking advantage of the poor man.

After his last court appearance he resigned from the local Operatic Society. Lewd comments from the audience had disrupted *The Pirates of Penzance*. After that, nightly sessions in CC's grew later and his rich baritone could sometimes be heard at two in the morning.

Spending less time at his practise, young customers deserted him. Managing to hold on to some of the older ones, especially those without young daughters, he just about stayed afloat. Never the less, whiskey, petrol, car repairs and contributing to the upkeep of four love children made wreck of his finances. His expenses grew and his income shrunk.CC gave him credit and his sisters helped out. To his credit, he never lost his nerve when lectured on the evils of drink.

"I know I am burning the candle at both ends old boy, but doesn't it shine brightly." Then one morning Henry's car gave up the ghost. "Too many encounters with stone walls old boy, the liquor always did make her skid."

The bank manager, a man of sober habits was remarkably unsympathetic. CC listened to his tale of woe. "A lot of useless pricks old boy; give you an umbrella when the sun is shining, then take it back when it rains. I am snookered; I need a miracle old boy."

Now, miracles are not unknown in Ireland. At this time, Maeve O'Hara, a rich American widow was touring in the area. Seeking her roots, she said, and determined to enjoy her widowhood. Her late husband had dropped dead whilst sweeping snow from his front step on the first day of his retirement. He had been a successful builder and made money quicker than his wife and daughter could spend it. With her daughter happily married in California, Maeve found herself at a loose end. Mourning Sam for the customary twelve months she then decided to live a little.

Well-groomed and in her early fifties, heads still turned when she entered a room. Tiring of her friend's efforts to play cupid and after a few messy affairs, she found New York was infested with free loaders eager to share her wealth and beautiful home. Despite being cosseted in her marriage, Maeve considered herself street wise and a complete break was needed.

Her grandparents had emigrated from County Galway and her late husband's ancestors had come from County Limerick. It would be nice to delve in to the past. Hiring a large American car at Shannon she created quite a stir when she drove into the little town of Carra. Taking some local children for trips along the coast road endeared her to the locals. They took her to their hearts even to the extent of claiming distant relationships. Maeve put up at Harts Hotel. It had a sort of faded grandeur, shabby chic, I think it is called. Frequented by the local hunting and fishing set, she soon joined the gin and tonic brigade in the bar each night. After about a week she confided in Jimmy the barman.

"Snobbishness is rife with that lot and they seem to have an inordinate love of killing little animals. I suppose they represent the types who took their children to witness public executions."

"Shure I know the type," Jimmy said, "tuppence halfpenny, looking down on tuppence."

"Well Jimmy, I prefer the company of thespians and artists and some real home grown characters."

Jimmy was slightly deaf but he offered her advice.

"CC's is different Mam, you might like to try it. I don't think there are lesbians but you will meet some piss artists and characters like you have never met before."

Intrigued by it all, Maeve decided to visit CC's that very night. It was a short distance from her hotel and she was aware she was swapping mahogany and carpets for rough deal tables and flagstones. CC's bar was packed when she entered and Henry was singing, the *Snowy Breasted Pearl*. Surrounded by his acolytes his rich baritone filled the room. Ex- doctor Teddy had woken from a drunken sleep. James, a failed politician, was gazing at Henry, and for the moment forgetting his woes. Larry, the street cleaner, was conducting an imaginary orchestra, and Liz Mac's mascara, awash with whiskey induced tears, was running down her cheeks. CC, our genial host, was topping up all empty glasses. There was magic in the air. Maeve gazed at Henry through a fog of whiskey fumes and tobacco smoke. She was smitten. Their eyes met and Henry our very own stud was in love again.

"Well the Lord protects her," said Liz Mac. "Little does she know that a cat's not safe going through a skylight with that ram."

Henry kissed her hand and was a model of decorum. With a large pocket handkerchief he dusted down a seat for her at one of the tables. He sent CC scurrying off to get one of his mother's Waterford cut glass crystal glasses. He certainly gave CC lessons in how to treat a lady. At the end of the evening he escorted Maeve back to her hotel and dutifully gave her a peck on the cheek. Impressed by his impeccable manners and old world courtesy, Maeve went thoughtfully to her bedroom.

This warm hearted generous woman soon discovered his Achilles' heel. Trying valiantly to wean him away from his favourite watering hole she organised all sorts of diversions. Cancelling her return trip to America, she rented a little love nest. There were theatre trips, sightseeing trips, and candle lit dinners. She drove Henry on his house calls to outlying farms and succeeded in upsetting his sisters.

"Those bloody Yankee women are pushy and domineering, and the poor love has never been subjected to that."

But Maeve had seen Henry in the early mornings. His hands shaking like ivy leaves and his teeth chattering like castanets. He was not a pretty sight before his first drink of the day. Sometimes at seven in the morning he grabbed her car keys and drove to CC's. Now CC's political career had suffered a setback at that time and they commenced their day with glasses of raw Paddy whiskey, or 'easy start', as Henry called it.

Maeve decided that to have any chance she had to take Henry out of his environment. They would both go to America. Henry was hesitant but he was also broke. They threw a party and announced their plans. People said it was the end of an era and there was sadness in the community. Their departure was witnessed by at least a hundred people. CC gave a speech his voice cracking with emotion. Liz Mac was in floods of tears and two of his four children turned up and blew kisses, despite the fact that Henry refused to recognise them.

Maeve and Henry boarded the train. Michael, the station master, waved the flag and was heard to exclaim, "Jasus it's like the Raj leaving India here this morning."

Henry's exile was brief. Emigrants seem to settle better when they are young and sober and Henry was neither. Never very forthcoming about the American experience, he returned alone inside of six months. Once more he took up his position on the high stool in CC's, as if he had never left. Now sporting a well waxed moustache, carrying a silver headed walking cane and dressed in a smart suit, he bought a car that had one careful owner. Liz Mac, a woman with amazing powers of deduction, maintained, that Maeve was so glad to get rid of him that she gave him a fistful of dollars.

CC was delighted to see his friend and mentor back, as at this stage he was in need of a lot of guidance. His sisters welcomed him back and even threw a party for the returned Yank.

He survived, and even pulled back some of his business. A distinguished looking man, he paraded the streets of Carra until his late eighties, always apologising for his forgetfulness and speaking with a slight trace of an American accent.

WHANG THE MILLER

"Mairead Ni Houlihan son."

"That's my auntie, sir; just around the corner you will see the sign, Eireoimid feasta, it's in the Gaelic sir, it means we shall rise again."

"I hope so son." He was on horseback; a beautiful roan mare. It was nightfall and it had begun to snow. Both horse and rider looked weary as they turned the corner. My news that Aunt Margreth had a visitor was greeted in silence by Mam and Dad.

I went to collect my dad's paper at the corner shop next morning. Miss Dooley, the priest's housekeeper, was holding court. With her long neck, pale face and pointed chin, she wallowed in trouble, gossip, and scandal.

"I'm telling you, I saw him with my own two eyes, rubbing down the horse, he was. Shure anyone would notice the prison pallor, and I'm led to believe he's an atheist." Conversation dried up as I entered the shop.

I went to my Uncle Jack to ask him about the man with the Northern accent. At that time I believed that Jack was like God and knew everything. Uncle just took off his cap and scratched his head. He answered me by quoting lines from a poem: "In to a town land, one night of snow, came a man from god knows where, none of us asked him to come or go, but we stabled his big roan mare."

When Uncle looked you straight in the eyes, you never pursued the matter any further.

A few days after his arrival, the stranger moved in to an old derelict mill house. There was no house warming party. Pushing the door off its rusty hinges, he lit a fire, and commenced to get rid of the resident vermin. Aunt Margreth gave him an old mattress, two bags of peat, some crockery and an old packing case, this would act as his bedside locker.

The local priest, Garda Siochana and all local busy bodies took a lively interest in his activities. In a matter of weeks he transformed the place. The water wheel was turning and he had restored the milling side.

Never introducing himself formally we called him Whang the Miller. I think the origins are from an old German folk tale. Working from dawn to dusk, he began to get a trickle of customers. Slowly he won the respect and affection of the community. Attending all wakes and funerals, the locals learned not to probe into his past. Those that tried met a steely gaze and a long silence. His accent showed he came from the North, and that had to suffice.

Before adding comforts to his home he built a comfortable stable for his mare. When she came in season she was serviced by a local expensive stallion, without charge. Showing an ambitious streak he tried to resurrect the kelp gathering industry. A very labour intensive job, seaweed is cut from the rocks, then dried and burnt, the by products are iodine and soda ash for the glass making industry. Unfortunately, he soon found these methods had been superseded during his absence from the commercial world. Emerging as a leader, he interested local farmers in flax growing. He designed and built a small scutching mill. The finished article was sent to the linen factories in Derry and Belfast. It lasted for about four years and then cheap imports put paid to the idea. Another defeat by circumstances beyond his control.

By this time he was tackling a host of repair jobs for the community. Having a tractor with wood cutting equipment and there being six large estates in the district, he was always busy. Families of wealth and influence offered him work as a day labourer. In the beginning he made it known that he would work on a contract basis only.

"Labour has commodity value," he said. "We stand as equals now; they need me as much as I need them."

However busy he was, Aunt Margreth's repairs were given priority. Despite his respect for her, she still frightened the hell out of me.

"I think highly of that woman. I just had her name when I came here, and she helped me when I was at the bottom of the barrel."

A rich Anglo Irish family gave Whang a lot of work. Lord Lordan, known as Holy Joe, walked his estate daily, reading his bible. He was not a popular man, and even the rooks did not nest in his woods. Uncle Jack told me the reason. On his way to Sunday service, a rook had defecated on his hat. This made him late, and he felt the rook had been prompted by Satan. Saturating a bucket of oats in poitin he scattered it on his lawn. When the rooks were too intoxicated to fly, he marshalled his staff and shot the lot. Rooks never nested in his woods again, not even to the present day.

Educated at Eton he was too small for the guards. Fulfilled by becoming the local magistrate, he issued five shilling fines to the locals for not having lights on their bikes. He kept himself aloof from us peasants, and his daughter, Lady Lucy, conducted business with the local trade's people. Whang seemed to get an inordinate amount of work from her. She was a blonde friendly woman with a rather chubby figure. They had a great interest in horses, amongst other things, Swiss finishing schools, and the political wing of the Curragh Prison seem a strange mixture, but the poets say, that love is blind when passions rule.

Whang got Lady Lucy in trouble, or in the pudding club as we called it. Holy Joe went berserk and threatened to shoot Whang. He was barred from any future contact with the lady and she was spirited away to Switzerland. This earth shattering news was not discussed in our house. Aunt Margreth was furious at Whang for fraternising with the enemy. Uncle Jack seemed the only one, who was delighted.

"It's the way forward boy," he said, "It breaks down the class barriers; the bed is a great leveller."

With his greasy old waistcoat, and puffing his pipe, he sat by his peat fire and saw a great future for our nation. Our own home grown egalitarian.

What happened to the child is shrouded in mystery. Lady Lucy returned after about twelve months and took up residence at the gate house lodge. For evermore she was banished from the big house and her father never spoke to her again; he also cut her out of his will.

Despite my Uncle Jack's hopes Whang and Lucy did not have a fairy tale end to their romance. Lucy soon went back to the bridge and tennis brigade. Travelling abroad quite a lot she died in France while still a young woman.

Whang never married and left suddenly at the beginning of the seventies. His goods and chattels were sold by public auction. A thousand words were said; plenty of theory and surmise, but even Miss Dooley failed to solve the mystery.

The Lordan's house is now a hostel, the gatehouse is an ivy clad ruin and Whang's mill house has changed completely. It has had a massive makeover. The wheel has been preserved. American dollars and a returned exile have made a big difference but the older people still refer to it as Whang the Miller's.

MORGANS MANSIONS

We called the brother's whitewashed cottage Morgans Mansions. It was just two up and two down and nestled in to the side of a steep hill. It was possible to run down the hill and spring straight on to their roof.

Finding this a great source of entertainment, we excelled ourselves by occasionally ramming down bundles of hay in their chimney. When they lit the fire the house filled with smoke and drove them gasping into the open air. Our little band of hooligans hid behind a fence and stifling laughter, watched the drama. Blaming wet peat, birds' nests and change of wind, they never once guessed at our blackguarding.

Knowing that James and Dick baked on Saturday mornings, one or two of our group always went to watch proceedings. Eventually sparks from the fire would set fire to the hay and they were able to proceed. I was fascinated by Dick's bread making. Unlike my mother, he never washed his hands before commencing. My mother wore a spotless white apron. Dick wore a badly frayed polo-necked jersey. This jersey was worn to milk the cow and to haul up his lobster pots in the bay. It was inevitable that cow hairs, fish scales and loose threads fell in the mix.

He commenced by taking a basinful of flour from a bag that was kept close to the fire. A shake of bread soda was added. This was pounded and kneaded whilst continuously adding splashes of sour milk. Shaped into a circle, with a cross in the centre, it was then placed in a bastable. When the fire was glowing after the trauma of a blocked chimney stack, hot embers were placed on the lid. The process was now under way. The timing of the cooking was by guess and by God. I never tasted the finished creation but it never killed them.

Since then, I have always believed that it takes a ton of dirt to kill you.

The brothers were like chalk and cheese. James was a tall, grim, taciturn man with sharp features and untidy side burns. He was twenty years older than Dick. Speaking no English, on the odd occasion when he wanted to communicate, it was through the medium of Gaelic. Dick was a short fat little man. Speaking both languages, he was reputed to be the biggest liar in Ireland, in both. All his experiences were embellished and dramatized. Now with the wisdom of hind sight I feel he fantasised more than deliberately lying.

Before the age of television I listened entranced to his stories. Whatever the subject, Dick had experienced, witnessed or excelled in it. He loved an audience and you were never allowed to doubt the veracity of his accounts. He had never travelled, yet he had spoken to kings and presidents. Ghosts were encountered weekly and he never differentiated between the living and the dead. From his lobster boat Dick had seen German submarines fishing for mackerel. Knowing for sure, that they came ashore to do their shopping, he had seen the name of a local hardware shop on one of their mackerel spinners. He told me that one evening he had seen a submarine blow the bows out of a hay boat. Looking quite surprised when I told him that I had never seen a hay boat, he told me they ferried hay to starving ponies in France.

Dick chewed tobacco incessantly and I could always track him, on the coast road, because of the tobacco spits. Our local priest said that he was fulfilling St Columcille's prophecy. The saint was reputed to have said that the human race would get small and would not be able to tell the truth.

After attending a political meeting Dick assured me that our little harbour would supersede Cobh as the venue for ocean going liners. I casually mentioned that our shallow draughted trawlers had problems negotiating our waterways. Gazing fiercely at me, he assured me that dynamite had been allotted to clear all those hazards. Sand and cement had been stored to create deep water anchorages. Tim and the president were the only people privy to this information.

Two acres of land, one cow and a lobster boat made up all the possessions of the brothers Morgan. These enabled them to scratch a living. To add a little money James was also the registered harbour pilot. The position did not carry a salary and so the income was spasmodic. Dutch and English cargo boats called infrequently. They brought us coal or timber and took away potters clay. Blasts from their fog horns heralded their arrival. They then hove too at the mouth of the harbour and awaited the arrival of the Morgan brothers.

When the siren sounded James and Dick burst forth with activity. James donned his badge of office. This consisted of a greasy seaman's cap and a navy jersey, frayed at the ends and with the letters HP printed across the chest. Dick prepared the lobster boat and they sailed off for their rendezvous with the incoming vessel. English ships presented few problems. Dick was able to act as interpreter and James had the knowledge of the deep water channels in his head. Maps were never mentioned, as Dick had told the authorities that they had lost them overboard. Finding those hidden treasures might have meant a loss of income.

Skippers were happy to have the brothers aboard. Tides were sometimes too low and this led to stress and confusion. You could almost hear the sighs of relief when at last they tied up at the jetty.

Despite Dick's sense of importance as an interpreter he was useless when it came to the Dutch captains. The captains usually spoke some English but once they tied the lobster boat to their sterns there was tension in the air. The Dutchmen were usually owners and captains, and sometimes had their wives on board. Sometimes they had all their families present. They wore clogs and the vessels were spotless. When James and Dick took over there was a sense of helplessness amongst the Dutch. Much sign language told the brothers to take off their shoes in the wheelhouse and they were always handed overalls to put on.

The four mile trip up the harbour probably took four years off the skipper's lives. Once tied up at the pier the vessel was handed back to the captain. Each land fall added to Dick's fantasies.

Neighbours were led to believe that James's presence was superfluous, and that he was the main man. He told me that in one period of great danger the captain's wife had clung to him. "Could not shake her off son," he said. "Clung to me like bad luck to a tinker's ass."

James died in the fifties. Despite lack of hygiene and their self-catering, he was healthy until the end. He had a traditional wake. Freshly shaved and in his best suit he was laid in his coffin. This rested on the kitchen table, which was placed in the middle of the kitchen. The neighbours walked around it and paid their respects. There were lashings of whiskey, tobacco and snuff. Dick, full to the brim and waxing eloquent would have us all believe that he would be canonised. There were no flowers or cards. Fishermen shouldered his coffin to the graveyard. On top was his old seaman's cap, the badge of his office. He was the last of the harbour pilots, the ships had stopped coming, there wasn't a need, and technology had moved us on.

Dick passed on in the seventies. His tales grew wilder as he aged. Along with kings and presidents, he now spoke to God. He had a direct line and did not need saints or priests as intermediaries. Cardinals and bishops sought his advice on cannon law, and for some bizarre reason he was convinced that the Pope was a Protestant. He had drawn a line and would not consult with his holiness. He died in his sleep surrounded by newspaper cuttings of celebrities. I missed his funeral, but visited Morgan's mansions recently.

Forty years on the little two up two down is an ivy covered ruin. October winds were howling mournfully through absent windows and doors when I walked up the overgrown path. Why did I call? It's off the main road. Did I expect to see James and Dick rush from the house, driven out by the smoke caused by a group of young hooligans?

COUSIN MOIRA

I visited cousin Moira last year. I think I was probably trying to step back. Maybe it was an attempt to make little of half a century. Then again, perhaps I needed to make my own mind up and cast aside all that I had heard over the intervening years.

Her family lived three miles from our village but they were oceans apart from us socially. We only met at large family gatherings and funerals. I gathered as a child, that they were rather posh and my parents were not impressed by some of the gossip that circulated.

Moira's mother died when she was very young. With Daddy being a successful business man, she was raised by a nanny and housekeeper. Daddy died when she was in her early teens. My parents were led to believe that pursuing ladies half his age contributed to his early death.

I remember Moira as a stunning looking blonde, with long, beautiful legs that seemed to go on forever. Graduating from university she carried on her father's business with a great deal of success. Moira also became a good amateur rider, a competent golfer, and trifled with local politics for a short time. My knowledge of my cousin in those years had all been obtained second hand. I gathered that she was a free spirit and lived a hedonistic lifestyle. Wild drinking parties, car crashes, and torrid affairs were all spoken of in hushed tones. One of the conversations I can recall went like this:

"It's in her, and breeding will out, but then God help her, she never had any guidance," this from my mother bent over the wash tub and up to her elbows in suds.

Then, from my father scraping out his pipe, "She's a lunatic on the road, a bitch on wheels." Then again, he disliked women drivers.

Moira married in her mid-fifties. A retired bank manager, completely unencumbered and with a liking for golf, and a paid up member of the gin and tonic brigade. They fought like cat and dog. On a wet afternoon in the golf club she poured out his short comings to the steward. He was the local agony aunt but eventually his patience ran out. "Why the hell did you marry him then?"

Moira answered without hesitation. "I was sick of other women's husbands, I wanted one of my own, and now I wish I had never bothered."

He died after about two years. Unhappiness and an enlarged liver ended that sad saga. Neighbours said that she donned her widow's weeds with a sigh of relief.

It was pouring rain on the evening of my visit. The entrance avenue was a quagmire. I knew she drove a Jeep, so I suppose potholes were not a problem. Two lovely ponies gazed over stable doors close to the house and two sheep dogs barked noisily as I rang the doorbell.

Moira was still a handsome looking woman. "Well hello Patrick, I heard you were about."

"I was passing and I thought I would say hello, we are distant cousins."

"Distant is the word," she said shaking my hand.

"Cead mile failte, sit up to the fire, you would not put a bad dog out this evening."

We sat in the kitchen. She fetched a bottle of malt from another room. Rain beat a tattoo on the windows. The open fire glowed. The level in the whiskey bottle dropped, and the years fell away.

"Your lot never approved of me much," she said.

"Moira, they were of that time, too busy being Catholic to be Christian and anyhow, I always felt you were a complete snob."

"We are all snobs in our way," she said. "People I know knew you in London in the sixties; they always said that you loved the smell of brandy and cigar smoke."

"Well Moira, I heard that you could have had the pick of any man in the county about that time. What held you back?"

"That's simple Patrick; those I loved did not love me, and those that did, I could not bloody stand. Anyhow, enough of that, you must be starving."

Explaining that she was not a domestic goddess, she rustled up a plate of sandwiches and a pot of coffee. We talked on until the early hours. We touched on her short-lived marriage. She poked the fire vigorously and put on some fresh coal.

"I had just retired Patrick, I was drinking heavily, and it was not fair on the poor man." Moira went on to say that most human beings had skeletons in the cupboard. "Shure, we all lose the way of ourselves from time to time darling."

She also went on to say, that it gets bloody cold in bed on your own in the mid-fifties. It was getting close to the dawn.

"You know you are always welcome to stay when you are around."

I felt I needed to walk back along the coast road. Every yard held memories for me. I listened to the waves crash onto the rocks below; a full moon shone on the harbour. In another life I had walked along here with a young wife and very much in love. Occasionally a cloud scudded across the moon. I felt I was alone on the planet. I wallowed in a bitter sweet wave of nostalgia; tears flowed freely.

The dark mood passed and I resolved never again to make judgements based on second hand gossip. Cousin Moira had accepted the hand of friendship. I had learned another lesson, and I knew from now on I would treasure the friendship of my elegant, feisty cousin.

REGATTA DAY

Regattas had been held for more than a century in our harbour. It was the biggest social event of the time. Mornings filled with great excitement and preparations. I would race from my bed to the end of the pier and watch as the great telegraph pole was put in place. It would stick out for seven yards from the end of the pier. Bags of sand acted as a counter balance and prevented it from tipping into the water. Large quantities of axle grease were then rubbed to the pole and a flag was attached to the end.

Everything in place for the fun event of the evening, this was billed on the programme as the Pig and Pole. The winning competitor would have to run to the end of the pole and snatch the flag. It led to great hilarity as the majority never made it and just toppled into the water.

The main event of the day would be the six oared gig race. Eight crews usually took part in this event. Each crew consisted of six rowers and a coxswain. They always arrived in lorries packed with supporters. The spoon blade oars would be lashed to the sides of the lorries and the gigs would rest on the top.

I can still see them as they placed the gigs reverently in the water. Late in the afternoon they would race four miles for the credit of their respective villages. We took great pride in our crews.

In the middle of the harbour the committee boat was anchored. She was a carefully scrubbed trawler, bedecked with flags and buntings of all descriptions. On regatta days she was always full to the gunnels with priests, judges, and dignitaries of all descriptions.

The starter and the judges were the only ones with a function to perform. A motor boat fussed noisily around the bay all day long. Their job was to arbitrate in the frequent disputes that took place. Most of these were caused by sailing dinghies especially when the weather was calm. They also ferried passengers and booze between the local hotel and the committee boat. There was always extravagant hospitality aboard and it was noticeable that the more important people wore life jackets, just in case.

About four in the afternoon the main event of the day took place. Eight six oar gigs lined up for the race everyone had come to see. The starting tape was a hawser running from the committee boat to the shore. The coxswains held on to this to ensure a level start. They would race towards a buoy two miles in the distance, turn around and row back to the tape. The starter's pistol was fired and this signalled the beginning of the struggle. A tremendous cheer went up from the supporters and forty-eight oars flashed in the afternoon sun. Wagers had been laid recklessly and men who had never held an oar in their life became instant experts. Along with their money, the honour of eight little villages along the coast was at stake. Loud speakers carried running commentaries and some lucky ones had binoculars.

Occasionally our local crew were the winners. All those years ago, I can still recall that great rush of pride and emotion. Pride in one's birth place, tribalism, call it what you will, it was a wonderful feeling to hear that victory roar echoing over the water.

Six oar gigs have largely vanished now. They had fixed thwarts and were believed to be a throwback to the British Navy. They would have been used to row the captains ashore. They would take the tillers themselves so there was no need for coxswains.

At six in the evening the local silver band would give a selection of 'Moore's melodies' and the crowds gathered at the basin of the pier. People wanted to get a good vantage point for the fun events of the day. Ice cream sellers lowered their price and did a roaring trade. Gypsy ladies with baskets full of liquorice and sweets roamed through the crowds. Hot dogs and chips were available from chip vans. Shouts from the vendors filled the air. All these gastronomic adventures, for a little boy with money in his pocket.

I cannot remember dodgems or chair-o-planes but a gentleman operated two swing boats close to the pier. These were basic. Two A frames and a cross bar. Two boats suspended and operated by the occupants by two ropes. It cost sixpence each ride and when the crowds were queuing he was quick to lift a four by two piece of wood and bring the momentum of the boat to a shuddering halt.

The evening program consisted of two swimming races, two pillow fights, two duck chases, and two greasy pole events. Senior and junior in each event, ladies were welcome but for some reason they never bothered. All this was in the forties; we even swam in different beaches.

The swimming races were taken quite seriously but the other events led to great hilarity. Two competitors sat on the greasy pole for the pillow fights .Whacking each other they usually pulled each other off the poll and ended up in the water. Somehow a winner emerged, usually covered in grease, feathers and scratches.

I always found the duck chase cruel. Swimmers lined up and chased the duck across the basin of the pier. I felt the duck was terrified as she strove to evade her captors. The winner caught the duck and held it aloft to the acclamation of some of the crowd; they would probably be the same people who enjoyed fox hunting and greyhound coursing. Thankfully that event is now illegal.

The finale was always the greasy pole event. A local man called Mickey Flynn was always our hero in this event. He drank steadily in the village pubs during the day. When he arrived in swimming trunks and sometimes unsteady on his feet he was greeted by a roar of approval. Insisting to the judges that a few jars steadied his nerves and improved his balance, he was popular with the villagers. A great bear of a man, black curly hair grew all over his body. The grease from the pole and the hair combined with a big belly gave him the appearance of a black seal as he came out of the water.

Standing by one of my neighbours one evening, I heard her say to another neighbour, "Would you look at his chest; it reminds me of the stuffing coming from a horse hair sofa."

We all willed him to win, which he did frequently. Singing a few verses of *Danny Boy*, he would grab his prize money and make a bee line for the nearest pub.

The shades of night were now falling and the local rook population had gone to bed. The last treat of the day was to watch the travelling strongman entertain the crowd. In the village square he danced to the band with a huge iron bound cart wheel balanced on his forehead. With his wife sitting on a chair he grabbed the rung in his teeth and circled the square to the cheers of the crowd. Naked to the waist he lay on a bed of nails whilst his wife grabbing a hammer broke stones on his chest. He rounded off the evening by pulling a bus against an incline. When his wife took up a collection, the people all gave generously. He had travelled the world, employed by the big circuses; he now preferred the freedom of the open road and the self-employed. I was really enthralled by his feats of strength and looked on him as a very glamorous figure.

My parents always sought me out about this time. I would have liked to linger and listen to the sounds of music and songs coming from the open pub doors. I had enjoyed a lovely day. I had eaten lots of things that were bad for me, but had avoided making myself sick as I had run out of money. One happy child needed no rocking that night.

A DAY IN THE BOG

A day in the bog was a must in every boy's life in the forties. With coal in short supply, peat was readily available but very labour intensive. Extra hands were always welcome. When I was about eleven I was asked to come along by two of our neighbours.

Mike Allan and Jimmy Hill entered into a discussion that morning; they found it hard to agree as to which of their animals was more suited to bog work. Mike's pony had the name of being giddy and work shy. He did not like to highlight this too much, as it would have an adverse effect at the next horse fair.

Jimmy had a mule. His flanks were lean, his eyes were sad and his age was shrouded in mystery. Eventually it was decided that the mule would be more sure footed for bog work. In the early morning sunshine we set off to harvest the peat. From the beginning I felt the mule was not enthusiastic and appeared to need an inordinate amount of persuasion.

Being a pessimist, on that morning I was full of grim forebodings. Feeling a little more cheerful when we arrived, I lit a fire; they had made it plain to me that I would be the cook. With the peat already cut and dried they began to shift some of it onto the roadside. This complete, they began to cut some more. During this procedure the mule began to graze. At lunchtime I boiled six eggs in a large kettle of water. The tea was made to Mike's instructions.

"Now listen lad, I like tea that you could trot a mouse across."

Using the water that I had boiled the eggs in, I added tea, sugar and milk. Boiling the concoction once more I was surprised when it tasted delicious. I am now told that this method is favoured in parts of India. Tea, brown home baked bread with masses of butter and homemade strawberry jam. Combined with hard boiled eggs and dining al fresco it was one of my most memorable meals.

During the meal break the owner of the bog paid us a visit. Casting a discerning eye over our activities, he inquired who owned the mule.

"It's mine, sir," Jimmy answered.

"I don't care who owns him," the bog owner answered, "but you must know, he should be dead years ago; he is a walking corpse."

My worst fears were now realised, as I knew this man's reputation as a judge of horse flesh, or in our case mule flesh. However when he left Jimmy's wounded pride knew no bounds.

"He is a know nothing fucker," he said stroking his steed lovingly. The mule bared his long yellow teeth, as if in agreement. I was not convinced. It was a warm day and the mule flagged noticeably in the heat of the midday sun.

Mike, as ever the soul of diplomacy drew our attention to the fact that mules have a reputation for being stubborn. By late afternoon our progress had slowed to a whisper and Mike mentioned that it might be best to tether the mule in the bog and that we would walk home. Jimmy would have none of it. He decided to load up the cart with some dry peat and topped it off with some bits of bog oak.

"Most of it is level ground," he said, "and anyhow that stuff is light as a feather."

With the sun moving to the west we began our journey home. It was decided that we would walk by the side of the cart to help matters along. The mule was showing his yellow teeth and breathing very heavily. Mike decided that we should stop at a way side pub after about two miles. A nose bag was placed on the mules head. Jimmy maintained that the rest and a feed of oats would set him up for the remainder of the journey. Mike, Jimmy and I then sat in the bar they quaffed foaming pints of Guinness and I sipped lemonade and wished that we were home.

There was laughter, cheer and witty stories, and the more they drank, the more relaxed they got. When the landlady lit the oil lamps, I think it dawned on them that we should be on our way. All the fun and laughter was short lived, because on leaving the watering hole, we found that the mule had lain down. He glared at us balefully and flatly refused to get up. My ingrained pessimism had been proved right.

Pub customers stood in groups. Offering advice and making stupid observations, they found the whole affair hugely entertaining. I was worried, Jimmy was angry and Mike was sweating profusely. However, come the moment, come the man, and man's greatest strength is in his greatest adversity. Big genial Mike emerged as a leader.

"Un-tackle him out," he said, "the road is fairly level from here until we get close to home."

We obeyed immediately and the mule got shakily to his feet. Mike got between the shafts and began to pull the heavy load. We left the pub to a lot of jeering and cat calls.

I can still see his whiskered face and huge walrus moustache as he strained to keep his burden on the move. Jimmy and I pushed, and the mule, shame-facedly, brought up the rear. The road was level for about a mile and a half and we made fair progress over that bit. Then we reached a gentle incline. This was not helpful. Mike was showing signs of distress. Sweat was dripping from his shiny red cheeks, and to Jimmy's great amusement he was also farting like a dray horse. The position was not improved by the insulting remarks made by the few passing motorists. He finally accused us of slacking and piss taking. Our little cavalcade finally came to a shuddering halt. Morale now at a low ebb, we were hungry fatigued and dejected.

Jimmy glowered at his forlorn old mule. "Maybe the old bastard has got his second wind," he said.

We tackled him in once more, and with three of us pushing we got to the top of the incline. At the summit the mule dropped his head and lay down once more. He had plumbed the depths of his strength and refused to offer any further assistance. Un-tackling him out once more, Mike got between the shafts. The road was downhill from there until we reached the corner at the bottom of our village. With the mule hitched to the back of the cart we helped Mike and prevented the cart from gathering too much speed. On reaching the corner at the bottom of our village, Mike fell forward on the shafts. He was completely exhausted. The moon was now high in the sky a steep hill leading to our homes put a stop to any further progress.

At this stage the pubs had turned out and we became the centre of attention. Full of Guinness and chattering like monkeys, a crowd gathered to witness our discomfiture. Jimmy was dispatched to borrow a pony from his brother in law. After what appeared ages, he returned with a pony and cart. Mike roused himself when he saw the cart.

"Why the fuck did you bring a cart? We already have one; it's a gun we need to shoot that shagging mule."

Angry words were exchanged, and sash windows were raised. People like to be up to speed when there is a chance of a fight. Peace descended with the arrival of a member of the Garda Siochana. He was a helpful man and after a consultation, he came back with a long rope. The cart with the peat was lashed onto the fresh pony and cart, and of course the old mule was still hitched to the peat cart. The last half mile commenced to a chorus of cat calls, boos, whistles and barking dogs. It was two in the morning before we unloaded the peat and fed the animals.

Speaking to Jimmy later he just said that peat harvesting was labour intensive. Never once did he concede that hiding the truth about a decrepit old mule had contributed to our fiasco.

SHIPWRECK

One dark foggy morning in December, a bearded man walked out of the gloom and collapsed at Maria Coleman's feet. Maria always rounded up her cattle for milking in the early morning. She legged it and leaving the cows called her husband Jimmy. Grabbing a hurricane lamp and taking his shotgun he went to investigate. Living in an isolated farm, and close to some dangerous cliffs, he left his wife and went to the cliff tops. His twelve year old son followed at a safe distance.

They found the stranger weak but lucid. He spoke in a foreign language and kept pointing to the cliffs at the bottom of the meadow. Jimmy's young daughter came on the scene and having learned French at school, she soon established that there had been a shipwreck and five men were still aboard.

The *Annette* lay on a ledge at the bottom of the cliff and was barely visible from the headland. Jean, the Frenchman had managed to climb a fifty foot cliff in a raging storm and on a foreign coast. It was now daylight, the rescue services had arrived and Jean was whisked off to hospital.

I missed school that day. I got into trouble later, but it was worth it. Who could sit in a classroom surrounded by so much drama? I joined the watching crowd and went unnoticed. The wind had dropped a little but the lifeboat pitched and rolled as she manoeuvred close to the rocks. The skipper was a cousin and one of my childhood heroes. The crew were also well known to me.

The SS *Annette* had lost her rudder off the Fastnet lighthouse, in a force eight gale. Her wireless also out of action, she had drifted helplessly towards the coast. She was ninety foot long, yet the Atlantic breakers threw her around like a cork. Eventually, she was driven, broadside on, and tossed on to a ledge. Despite the flying spray we could see her crew on deck, and the gaping hole on her port bow. Looking at her stern the propeller was also missing. The cruel sea had shown her no mercy.

The lifeboat crew, using their bow gun, got a line aboard the stricken trawler. With the line the trawler crew were able to pull a hawser aboard. This meant that a breeches buoy could be rigged. This equipment is basically canvas trousers with brass rings attached. This is roped up to a pulley and can be pulled to and fro. The hawser was tied to the trawler's mast and the other end to the lifeboat's mast. Five men now depended on this contraption for their lives.

Watching with bated breath while the first man was pulled, there was a little cheer as he was pulled onto the lifeboat. The seamanship was superb. If the hawser dipped too much in the centre, they would drown the man they were trying to rescue.

After about four hours the rescue was complete. The lifeboat departed, and five exhausted Frenchmen were en route to hospital. The watching crowd dispersed, all impressed by the bravery and skill of a lifeboat crew. All volunteers, all unpaid.

Jean had discharged himself from hospital and surrounded by a bunch of reporters in the local hotel, was drinking pints of Guinness. Making light of his achievement he was feted as a hero for several days. Later, it turned out that, luckily, rock climbing had been one of his hobbies.

I left the cliff top, as it was getting dark. The *Annette* looked so deserted down there with only the seagulls for company. I visited her daily after that and one calm day my uncle took me in his yawl so as we could view her close up from the sea. All kinds of sea birds flew in and out of the gaping hole in her bow. "That will be her grave yard now boy," he said. Events were to prove him wrong.

The trawler owners arrived from France with expensive looking Crombie overcoats, highly polished shoes, Gallic shrugs, and lots of hand waving. They sounded angry, but was it just a strange language? They left quickly in their hired limousine. I did hear Lloyds of London mentioned. "She is nobody's child now," Mrs Coleman said. Two days later the man from Lloyds arrived.

Carrying a Gladstone bag, with his dark overcoat, striped pants and bowler hat, he was the most impressive figure I had seen up to then. He certainly resented having to walk across a muddy field to view the *Annette*. It was raining heavily as he tentatively gazed over the cliff edge. Holding his umbrella in his right hand he scratched his head and scuttled back to the warmth of Mrs Coleman's kitchen. Opening his Gladstone bag he scribbled something on an important looking document. Refusing hospitality he made a bee line for his taxi and rushed back to the city. With a few scratches of his pen the SS *Annette* was now a wreck.

She lay there for the rest of the winter, her plates now rusting and sea birds using her deck as a resting place. I looked over the cliff edge frequently during that winter and always felt a great sense of sadness.

Jimmy and Peter Jones were cousins. They both owned trawlers. Another thing, they were both optimists, and that is rare for sea faring people.

"It's a terrible thing to see a lovely vessel lying there, like a beached whale," Jimmy said in the local pub one Saturday night. "If we could patch her up enough to get her to the shipyard, we could pull her off the rocks the next high spring tide."

Reading *Old Moore's Almanac* they were able to work out the dates. The patching would have to be makeshift. Skilled local welders would not risk their lives on such a hair brained scheme. Peter used all his powers of oratory.

"Join us, and if we win we can all make a lot of money. She just needs some plates welded and new propellers." Doubts were cast on their sanity and no interest was shown.

Jimmy and Peter pressed on. During calm periods they ferried materials onto the ledge where the trawler lay. A farm gate, three old bed springs and a ton of sand and cement. Their working conditions were atrocious. Sea spray washed over them at all times and of course our local pessimists said, "This is not going to work." Some of the more spineless ones did not want it to work.

Slowly, they made a rough patch. It was not pretty, but hopefully with a calm day, a high tide, and both bilge pumps working, they could pull her off the ledge. They would tie both their trawlers to the *Annette*. Taking up the strain they would position crew members at the sterns. They would be armed with axes. If anything was to go wrong they would slash through the connecting hawsers.

When the chosen day arrived the sea was like a milk pond. The sun shone and it was the highest spring tide we had ever seen. The local priest said that the Lord had blessed the enterprise. The national radio station had hired a motor launch to watch proceedings.

I did not have to bunk off school as it was a Saturday. The cliff tops were crowded with sightseers. At eleven o clock both trawlers threw their engines to full ahead. With a groan and a shudder and to a wild burst of cheering, the *Annette* floated off the ledge. It was somewhat of an anti-climax. We lost sight of her as she was towed around the headland. A man with binoculars said that she was down at the bows and must be shipping water. Later we were told that she barely made it to the dry dock. The patch had leaked like a sieve and one of the bilge pumps packed in. The men stationed on the sterns had axes at the ready. Jimmy and Peter had kept the men's morale high. The promise of large bonuses also helped.

Fishermen seldom learned to swim in those days. Like the gold ring in their right ear, this was tradition. If they fell overboard they wanted to die quickly and the gold ring was to pay for a Christian burial if washed up on a strange shore.

The *Annette* sailed from the ship yard three months later. Now called the *St Christopher*, she was bought by an African state and became the biggest vessel in their fleet. Called after the patron saint of travellers, I hope she bounded over the blue for many years after that and avoided any more cruel mishaps.

AUNTY BARBARA

When Barbara stepped from the train, I clasped my mother's hand and wondered why some men on the platform seemed to draw in their bellies and stand a little straighter. My mother and Barbara hugged each other and laughed through their tears. Running her fingers through my hair, Barbara kissed me.

It was my first time seeing a returned Yank. Her perfume did not smell of violets like the one my mother used and the seams on her nylons were straight. She carried just one suitcase, did not have much of an accent, and seemed to question my mother about everything that had happened in the eight years of her absence.

Babs, as we called her, knew about life and the hard knocks that are sometimes dealt out. Orphaned at ten and with my mother, who was her younger sister, they had to grow up fast. Losing their small farm, they escaped the orphanage due to the good graces of a kindly aunt.

A young age Babs left to make her fortune in America. In later years she told me that she had one dream. It was to make enough money to buy back the farm they had lost and to assuage the great land hunger that stayed with her until the day she died.

Fools were never suffered gladly. With her piercing gaze, strong features and flaming red hair, she always had plenty of admirers. People said that she never left the same street in Boston during her eight years there. Working during the day as a self- employed cleaner, she spent her evenings working at a gas station. Most of this money was saved, except for a small sum she sent to her Aunt.

Seeking a man with land, she let it be known that she would come with quite a large dowry for the time. Marrying a man twenty years her senior, she moved in to his home and overcame all opposition from his doting mother. It was no contest. Soon the old woman moved in to a smart new house in the local town. Babs with passion and single mindedness, set out to put a largely neglected farm on the map. They prospered, and three bouncing boys followed in quick succession.

Her childhood farm came up for auction. The bidding against her was scant and half-hearted. When the gavel went down she rushed from the room and walked every field on the farm.

"It was lost and now it is found again," she said.

Shortly afterwards she encouraged her husband to buy a trawler. He was inspired by this go ahead woman and it also gave employment to six local men. Working twelve hour days she increased the dairy herd on her two farms. Increasing her acreage by bidding for every bit of land that came up for sale, the local bank manager always doffed his hat when he met her on the street.

It became obvious to neighbours that the animals on her farm were better housed than the family. It took all her husband's powers of persuasion to convince her of this. Eventually she walked the length and breadth of her land to choose a site for the new homestead. In her heart she felt that it was shameful to cover fertile land with yards of concrete. After great soul searching, a barren, rocky piece of scrub land was chosen. Even then architects and builders had to use all their diplomatic skills. The breakthrough came when her husband conceded that the house would be restricted to four bedrooms and the old house would be converted to a milking parlour.

"This will be the least wasteful of our options," she said.

Joe her husband died of cancer before the completion of the project. Wearing black at his funeral, this was to be her mode of dress for the rest of her life. Two farm labourers were hired immediately and now eight employees and three children depended on her efforts.

In an era when most women stayed in the kitchen, Babs was not found wanting. Bills were paid on time and wages paid on the spot. Her little empire was run without an office, or any of our present day gadgetry. Three note books and a shiny black handbag seemed enough for this no nonsense woman. Low overheads enabled her to buy another trawler and add another small farm to her holding. She was now indeed a woman of substance.

As a child, she once told me that our richness was in the fewness of our needs. Her personal needs were few. One luxury, a beautiful high stepping roan mare. Tackled to a tub trap and arrayed in a glistening harness, the mare proudly conveyed her mistress to church on Sundays. Sitting in the trap in her familiar black and surrounded by her three well-scrubbed sons, she looked a picture.

I got the feeling that she was not a great believer in love and romance. Neither do I think she was short of offers of both from young men with their eyes on the main chance.

"Fancy words and blarney never bought a new dress for the baby," she said to my mother. "Shure if you turned some of them upside down and shook them, all you get is a bit of loose change."

Childhood and her early years in Boston must have left some insecurity. Wealth accumulated but nothing was spent on outward show. Money was ploughed back in to her farms, her trawlers, and her staff was always well paid. She did educate her sons but during their time home from university she made sure that they worked on the farm, always making sure that they had a project to carry on with. I sometimes think that she regretted her own lack of education.

"I just had the basics," she said, "but the Lord gave me plenty of common sense." That she had in abundance and could spot a charlatan or phoney a mile away.

Age brought its own infirmities but she still held the reins of power. Her sons would not change their shirts without referring to mother. The old matriarch certainly ruled the roost in that house. Her son's girlfriends were warned off with alarming regularity.

An intelligence unit had emerged amongst toadies in her workforce. Due to this state of affairs three strong men became silent, secretive and most probably emasculated.

Shortly before her death she had called the local undertaker. Sitting on a chair at the end of her bed, he carefully wrote down her instructions: the cheapest coffin in his range, a simple headstone over her grave, and just her husband and her name on it. When he told her the lettering on the headstone cost so much per letter, she told him to forget about their ages.

"I am so glad I have that done," she told a neighbour. "Those lads of mine would be talked in to spending hard earned money for something that is as natural as being born."

She could not rule from beyond the grave. On her death, her sons behaved like rudderless ships. An office was opened in town. A manager was hired. Of course each of them had to have a secretary. Office machinery and shed loads of paper seemed to appear from nowhere. In a couple of years, without expansion, the little empire had accumulated a lot of useless appendages.

Some of the old fishermen shook their heads and said it would probably be clogs to clogs in two generations. Her eldest son Joe had trained as an accountant, and was the first to get a wake-up call.

The fifties were not good for fishing or farming, the whole company had a reality check. In a time honoured fashion there were cut backs and slowly the company came back on course. They moved into timber and coal importing and began to make some real money. They distanced themselves from the company and began to employ proper managers.

They change their BMW's frequently now, and the Cheltenham festival is a must every year. They are dour, soft spoken men. They never married. Probably not a woman on the planet who could come up to mother's standard.

HAIRY TOM

Hairy Tom was a daylight atheist. His eccentricities were numerous, and with all the cruelty of children, we were forever teasing him. Standing six foot six inches, he had the longest legs I have ever seen on a man. He had long hair and sideburns and his face always seemed too small for his head.

When he came into the village for his groceries, he seemed to overshadow the small donkey that he rode. On finishing his shopping, he balanced his two shopping bags on the donkey's neck. He then sort of walked on to the donkey, as his long legs still reached the ground. As they set off his legs kicked up little clouds of dust from the road. As children, we felt that he was using his shoes as brakes. We called him 'bomb bombs'. When an aircraft flew overhead he shouted, "take cover," stepped off his donkey and cowered in the water table until the plane passed over. A passing motor bike brought on the same reaction. The donkey seemed to understand as he always stood and waited patiently.

Living in a little cottage owned by the Church of Ireland minister, he rang the bell for services and kept the yard clean and tidy. Carrying out his tasks conscientiously, it was strange that he believed in none of it. Rumour had it that he had been the minister's batman in the First World War. It was known that the minister had embraced religion after the trenches; it seemed to have the opposite effect on Hairy Tom.

Too old for the Second World War, Tom avoided newspapers and radio broadcasts like the plague. When neighbours mentioned happenings from the scenes of war, his stock answer was always "News to me."

Tom was popular, and he helped at threshing, haymaking, and turf cutting. Being friends with the local priest, he also helped him in his garden.

His greatest interest however was the minister's flock of pedigree goats. The minister was a big supplier of goat's milk in the locality. There was always a ready market as lots of people believed in its medicinal properties. Tom was dedicated to the care of the flock. There were ten in all and they all had names. Tom called them by their names at milking times and he recognised each and every one of them. Running happily in the wood at the back of the minister's house, they all had bells on their necks. It was always pleasant to sit on still evenings and listen to the jingle of the bells as they grazed happily.

At six every morning he took his flock a special treat. This concoction was his secret, but he maintained that it increased milk yield and increased their desire to breed. It must have been successful as the local vet never had to visit his flock.

One Sunday morning at six Tom discovered that one of his flock called Maria was broody. Informing the minister of the position and putting a lead around the skittish Maria's neck, Tom set out to take the goat to the buck.

Paul Edmonds, the buck's owner lived on a little hill farm about three miles away. November is the rutting season, and when they arrived the buck was busy. Paul informed him that his charges had increased and he would have to let Maria stay overnight. Tom had no option, as pedigree bucks were in short supply in the locality. Thoroughly disgruntled and with rain teeming down, Tom set off for home. Knowing he had to repeat the trip the next day and being too late to ring the bell for the morning service added to his angst. When he got opposite the church, there was a terrific peal of thunder. Shouting, "Take cover," he rushed to the shelter of the church porch.

The service had reached the sermon part, and John, the minister, his grey locks neatly parted and his arms outstretched, was in full flow, the subject being Paul's letter to the Corinthians. With his deep public school accent, and fervour, his congregation were always very attentive. As Tom sheltered in the porch, the minister paused for breath and to give his audience time for reflection. Commencing once more he said in a loud voice, "And what did Paul say?"

"He said Maria would have to stay overnight, and he would buck no more goats for two shillings, it was a half crown from now on or no service," Tom piped up.

The reverend was taken aback and the youngest of the Heflin sisters burst into hysterical laughter. Tom realised that he had got it wrong and left the church in great confusion.

Like everything else it was only nine days' talk, despite being a great source of merriment, as it was told, retold, and embellished.

Tom began to lose it a bit as he aged. The old war wound played him up and he was liable to take cover at the least noise. After a lecture at school our little gang ceased teasing him and shouting 'bomb bombs'.

His donkey long dead and the minister and his goats moved to a parish in the midlands, Hairy Tom was taken into care. Living out his life in the calm atmosphere of a home run by the nuns, his nerves improved and his health got better.

Towards the end of his life he helped in their vegetable garden and farm. Very impressed by their kindness and care, he converted to Catholicism near the end. The minister came back to our village for his funeral. At the graveside I heard him say, "I always felt he was a daylight atheist; I met very few atheists in the trenches."

As an adult and after learning of the madness and slaughter of the First World War, I regret ever having teased him. The cruelty and thoughtlessness of youth...

LEAVING HOME

Fastnet Engineering went broke in 1953. I found myself half trained, half tamed and quite confused. What did the future hold, and where to go?

Mr Giles, my boss, did his best. He gave me a letter of introduction to the parent company in Kensal Green, West London.

"Stick it out for another two years lad, and you will be a skilled engineer, it may be tough at times but a trade will stay with you for the rest of your life."

London sounded exciting, and two days before my seventeenth birthday, I left Cork Harbour on the SS *Inisfallen;* my first time on a ship and joining the great exodus of the fifties. I was an emigrant but at seventeen there is a great sense of excitement, and after all, the streets of London are paved with gold.

Paddington station sixteen hours later was quite a culture shock. There was a freezing fog and the smell of sulphur from thousands of coal fires, and people rushing in all directions and station announcers, with strange metallic sounding voices. Then there were the notice boards, with times and destinations, continuously clicking and changing. The noise was almost unbearable and the people all had a strange yellow pallor on their faces. There were lights everywhere, even though it was the middle of the day. And strangest of all, a man on his knees polishing peoples shoes. This indeed was a strange country.

A kindly gentleman told me how to get to Kensal Green W10. The underground was speed like I had never known it. I got off at Westbourne Park and found the factory quite easily.

Jock McLarren was seated at an impressive looking mahogany desk with a green leather top. He was a Dickensian looking character with a florid face adorned with huge side burns, and meaty hands clasped and resting on a well-nourished belly. He had a turned down pipe clenched between strong white teeth, and a tweed jacket draped over the back of his chair. The desk was clear, just a phone, a paper knife, and a fountain pen and note pad. I thought of old Mr Giles desk, always cluttered and with invoices spilling on to the floor.

For the first time, I felt a pang of loneliness. Jock read my letter of introduction, and shook my hand. His grip was firm, and I immediately took a liking to the man.

"Sit down laddie; you must be tired and hungry."

"Thank you sir, I am hungry and I am not a good sailor."

"I know the feeling laddie; I was on the trials of the *Hood.* I sailed as chief engineer for four years and I was always sick first night at sea.

"Miss Hunt, get the lad a few ham rolls and two mugs of strong tea."

She obeyed and even managed a frosty smile.

"I hope you settle in OK laddie, old Giles speaks highly of you. Take tomorrow off to sort yourself out and report to Mick May on Monday morning."

I grabbed my travelling bag and left the presence of the boss man.

It was now thirty six hours since I had been to bed and I still had not sorted out a place to stay. With a great sense of loneliness and probably a bit of panic, I entered the bar of the King's. A blazing coal fire, shiny mahogany and a large whiskey took chill and panic from the evening. Sitting by the fire, I drifted off to sleep, comforted by accents from the four corners of Ireland.

"Wake up my son this is not a doss house," a well-built blonde lady shook me awake. "Time to go home son."

I explained that this could be a problem and apologised for falling asleep.

"It's half ten, love and you will find difficulty getting in anywhere at this time of night. If you hurry you will get the last train to Hammersmith, and Rowton House will admit until midnight."

I dashed for the train and found the building close to the station. A sad faced old man sat at reception. Staring at me knowingly he said, "Just docked then son and already a guest of Lord Rowton. It's two shillings for a cubicle and five shillings for a private room. If you have no money, I just want your name and you do not have a choice. Tea, bread and marge is served at seven and you have to vacate by eight."

I paid five shillings and collected two blankets and a pillow. Lord Rowton's hostel did not run to sheets or luxuries of any kind. The rooms were clean but there was a smell of Jeyes fluid everywhere. The walls were paper thin and all sounds were amplified on the stone corridors. I fell asleep but was awakened shortly afterwards. The pubs had emptied and a huge influx of people was stamping about in reception. The sad old gentleman in reception was using all his powers of diplomacy to get the unruly hoards settled for the night. Scottish, Irish, Welsh, and Geordie accents were easily distinguished. Frequent arguments, occasional singing, and shouts and mumbling went on for what appeared hours. A furious row broke out in the early hours. Michael in reception had barricaded himself in, but still managed to calm down the hooligans.

I wished I was back in my own bed in Ireland, being lulled to sleep by the Atlantic breakers, which were a short distance from my bedroom window. Eventually I fell into an exhausted sleep.

A loud bell rang at seven and there was a stampede for the wash house, and the hatch where tea, bread and marge were being served. I dressed quickly, skipped breakfast, and walked into the wintry sunshine of Hammersmith Broadway. Eating a hearty breakfast at a Lyons corner house, I took the train back to Westbourne Park.

I sought lodgings for some hours without success. Slightly panicky by now and fearing that I would have to stay another night with Lord Rowton, I adjourned to the King's in the Harrow Road. Maria, the pub landlady, greeted me and thought it was hilarious when I told her of my restless night. I was spellbound as I watched her in fits of laughter, as three rows of pearls bounced up and down on her ample bosom.

"Speak to Mrs Doyle in the saloon bar, she may point you in the right direction," she said, getting her breath back.

I picked up my holdall and entered the rarefied atmosphere of the saloon bar. This was the era of the caste system amongst the drinking classes. You had the bottle and jug for take away, the public bar for men in working clothes, and the saloon bar for people who could afford to dress well and pay two pence more per drink. Kathleen Doyle and a cluster of local lodging house keepers were having some lunchtime gin and tonics. Maria made the introductions and I stated my case.

Kathleen, dressed in black, large chested, wide of hip and slender of waist, had more paint and powder on than the Mona Lisa. Wearing lots of jewellery, including on her ankle, I got the feeling that she jangled when she walked. Wearing her hair in a beehive, and with her red pouting lips, she looked amazing and I had never seen such a striking looking woman in my life. Up to then the women in my life, including my mother, had always dressed in a very sedate fashion. Offering me a drink, she took a packet of Craven A from a large shiny black handbag, lighting up a cigarette and screwing up her eyes against the smoke, she made a decision.

"I am quite crowded at the moment love, but I guess I can make room for a little un. I charge £3 per week full-board, four beds to a room. Sheets are changed weekly and food is first class. "Can you afford that? I know apprentices do not get a lot of money."

I hoped I could. I had left home with twelve pounds and my wages would be fifteen pounds per month. I paid her for one week and she immediately bought a round of drinks. I quickly learned that the landladies of W.10 were cash rich, and were mostly good natured, heavy drinking ladies.

We left the King's at three o' clock, and made our way to Kathleen's house in Kensal Green. Giving me a key, she showed me my room, and told me that my roommates were all Irish and were at work. It was large with a high ceiling. Four beds, four lockers and four wardrobes were placed strategically around the room. A Formica covered table and four chairs graced the centre of the room.

Owning the house next door, Kathleen had eight of these rooms as they were four storey houses with basements and Kathleen lived in one of the basements. A dining room and kitchen were on the first floor of one house.

I got into bed and slept luxuriously between clean sheets. Waking next morning to the smell of frying bacon, I had a nice breakfast. It was Sunday and Kathleen told me where the church was. I met my three roommates for the first time - two bricklayers from Dublin and a tunnel worker from Kerry. The house had a nice atmosphere and I felt at home, especially when I was in the King's.

I liked Kathleen from the beginning. I heard her describe me as an unspoilt country boy. She was kindness itself to me and that helped me cope with the early years. Her husband had left her some years before for a younger model; they had no children and she devoted herself to the running of her business. She was light hearted and bubbly and we soon became good friends.

THE NEW BOY

My first morning. Clock cards were in neat rows, all in a brown timber cabinet. They all had printed numbers. Mine was the last in the row and had been written in pencil. There was a satisfying clunk and a ringing noise as I clocked in and joined Kensal Engineering.

Mick May, who was to become my foreman, stood in the middle of the workshop, a tall grey-haired man with a twinkle in his eye. He was surrounded by a shower of sparks when I first saw him. De-burring some metal components on a rickety old grinding wheel, and oblivious to the din from a faulty bearing, he noticed me standing at my allocated bench. Removing his rigger gloves he came towards me with outstretched hand.

"You must be Patrick," he said, "I was told to expect you." I gave him my log book and he went off to speak to Jock McLarren. Returning, he told me that they had worked out what stage I was at.

"Have a walk round Patrick, make yourself known, we do not stand on ceremony here."

The boiler house and the welder's bench were side by side. The welder was a Liverpool Irishman and was well respected by all his work mates. His name was Jim Shacles and he also doubled as a blacksmith. I later found out that he had been a Prisoner of War during the war but unlike others never spoke of it. He took me under his wing that first day. He brewed strong tea on his furnace almost on the hour. The rest of us had two ten minute tea breaks and an hour for lunch. Behind his canvas curtains, he repaired all manner of things. High or low pressure vessels, copper, aluminium or steel held no terrors for him, and I was really impressed when he showed me the argon arc equipment, and this was to deal with stainless steel welding and was new technology to me. A steam whistle sounded at ten and I was introduced to the British tea break. A stern faced lady arrived with a tea urn and a barrow with ham, cheese and sausage rolls. Greeted by shouts of "Tea up!" she poured tea, dished out rolls and took the money. Most of the enamel mugs were chipped because of her rough handling, and she looked like a bulldog that had bitten on a piss soaked nettle. Her one eyed husband operated the tricoetylene tank that stood in the corner of the workshop.

Always in a foul mood, she felt that others should take a turn at the tank; Jim did not want a change as he was Trico happy. Trico boils at about ninety degrees Celsius, and the fumes rising from the liquid are effective at cleaning metal components. This chemical is also used in dry cleaning shops. Cold water pipes are fitted around the tops of the tanks, and when the hot vapour hits the cold pipes, it condenses and falls back in to the tank.

In the course of his work Jim inhaled this witch's brew all day long and legend had it that he took a bottle of it on his annual holidays. He slept soundly each lunch time. Lying on his bench, he always had his good eye closed, but the lid never closed over his glass eye and it stared into the distance.

Lorna, his tea lady wife, worked in the kitchen over the work shop and threw a sandwich over the railings when he woke. His work mates christened his place of work 'the bear pit' and cruelly christened him 'Wonk eye'.

By means of a block and tackle he lowered components in to the tank and then laboriously hauled them out. The only time the tedium was broken was when he changed the liquid and cleaned the tank. After this operation, his eyes were always glazed, and he seemed to walk as if he could not feel the ground. He refused all offers of a transfer. Twenty years later it was discovered that his job had a high health risk. He had departed by then, probably suffering withdrawal symptoms.

Mick May had warned me not to upset Jock McDaid. He ran the boiler house like a ship's engine room. Jim Shackles referred to him as Gladys. Keeping the door to the boiler house locked, he actually flounced when I knocked one morning.

"Mr McLarren told me to ask your permission to look around and become familiar with the steam raising plant. I am Patrick, the new apprentice."

"Come back after lunch, it is inconvenient at the moment. Give me that boiler suit, and I will repair it during lunch."

This was certainly strange, but I did as requested. I returned after lunch, the repair was complete, and he was knitting. Despite being coal fired the place was spotless. His rakes, pokers and shovels were hanging on a rack, and they were polished until they shone. The floor was painted, the copper work glistened, and everything was dusted daily. Two beautifully maintained boilers stood in the middle of the floor. Coal came from a hopper at a higher level and was shovelled on to the furnace. One boiler was steaming at 150 lbs per square inch and the other was undergoing its insurance inspection. The ancillary equipment looked well cared for, the boiler feed pump, the ash crusher and the hot well were painted with heat resisting paint and everything looked a picture. In the corner stood a sliding vane compressor that supplied the air for combustion. Jock came in at five in the morning and never left before five in the evening.

Jock went shopping every morning at nine and was delighted to pick up shopping for any of his work mates. Left largely to his own devices, he cooked and ate all his meals in his own mess room. Doing his washing on Mondays, he hung it over the boilers to dry and ironed in the afternoon. At one time, he wanted to bring in a bunk bed and live there, but despite having sailed with one of the directors this was turned down. He sulked for a while and got lodgings close to the works gate. A bachelor, non-drinker or smoker, he was reputed to be as wealthy as the Aga Khan. He was always disgruntled when he had to request help from the work shop fitters - they usually made a mess, ribbed him unmercifully and forced him to hide his knitting patterns and copies of woman's weekly.

The test and calibration room was next to the boiler room and I was destined to spend three months there. A crabby, disagreeable little man called Ron was my mentor. I suppose I was a nuisance, as he had to explain things to me and he disliked my light hearted approach when I got things wrong.

He had quite a responsible job and had to sign his name to jobs before they left the works. Safety valves are set to lift at twelve and a half per cent above the working pressure of a boiler. When controls fail they are the last line of defence. If they fail it is always a catastrophe, and only when I was older and had seen the result of these explosions did I realise why Ron gave himself ulcers.

After a service the valves were bolted on to a manifold and worked on until it discharged steam at the set point, this operation always caused a dreadful noise and frightened the life out of the anglers on the canal bank.

When Ron asked me one day what action I would take if I was duty engineer and one of those valves failed to discharge, he expected an answer straight from the text book, as he knew I attended college. When I said, "I would shut off the fuel supply, shut down the combustion air fans, sound the alarm, put a napkin between my legs and run," he laughed for the first time in my presence. I learned a lot from Ron and we were friends when I left.

The machine shop was quite small. It had all the necessary metal working machines. I did not have to spend time here as I had already covered that part of the course.

I was now shown the department where I would spend six months and where the most difficult skills would be imparted. The door said DEVELOPMENT OF PATTERNS AND PROTOTYPES. This department was run by Jim Patterson; I noticed the burns on his hands and the copy of the *Daily Worker* next to his sandwiches. Joe had flown as a tail gunner during the war. A Belfast man, he welcomed me warmly and never spoke about his experiences during the war. His bench was about half the size of a snooker table and was covered with green baize. Templates of all sizes and shapes hung on the walls. I told him that I was apprehensive about this aspect of the job. He went to Mick May and read up my log, and when he returned, he thanked me for my honesty, and he knew now at what stage he should begin to teach me. He was brilliant; a practical man, he made everything come alive. Parallel lines and triangulation began to lose some of their mystery.

"It's to do with vision lad; we cut it correctly on the flat, and then we shape it as the metal workers and tinkers of old did. We have the gear, don't wallow in it, shout for help when you need it, never get bogged down. I will get you through this and turn you into a craftsman."

Guillotines, rollers, benders, jenny wheels, rotary cutters, swaging tools, riveting and seaming tools, spot welders and gas welders, Jim built my confidence. Starting off with simple cones, then the transition pieces, square to round elliptical to round, solid block corners, lobster back bends, offsets and then one day I developed and made a breeches piece on my own. Jim ran his expert eye over it.

"That's it son, take command of the metal, it is inanimate and you have a brain."

The pages of my apprenticeship log were filling. Mick May came to talk to me every week. I told him, that drawings were my weak point, so he contacted the technical college and the lecturer spent a bit more time at my elbow. Mick also helped by giving me some time with the draughtsman.

McLarren summoned me to his office one afternoon. "Patrick, as an addition, I would like you to take The Boiler Operator and Insurance Certificate; I know this will be useful to you later on. It will mean a lot of theory and spending some time in the boiler house. Are you OK with that?"

I told him, that I had no problems with his plans, and I knew this additional certificate would be advantageous. Puffing his pipe furiously, he gazed at me, "You have met McDaid?"

"I have sir." I could see he was ill at ease.

He cleared his throat. "Now Patrick," he said, "when McDaid prays at night, he gives thanks that he is not like the rest of men."

"I am aware of that sir."

"That's fine then, as you will have to put up with some leg pulling from the workshop." McLarren looked relieved when I left his office

The following Monday, I knocked at the door of McDaid's kingdom. Workshop wags had advised me to bring in my laundry and any shirts that had buttons missing. I ignored this advice but I was apprehensive. The bolts were withdrawn.

"Wipe your feet. I have some tea and toast ready."

A second chair and a flowery mug had been added to his mess room. Whilst sipping his tea, he told me that we had to get off on the right footing and he was going to lay down a few ground rules,

"I would like you to continue using the work shop showers. One of your colleagues, the filthy man, I foolishly let him use the boiler house shower, he left pubic hairs everywhere.

"I do not want you to do any cleaning, none of you can.

"I do not want you washing the tea things and please leave your horrible enamel mug out of my boiler room. When you use the roller towel please move it on. I go shopping at nine every morning, and can pick up anything you may need. Last but not least, do not enter the mess room with your work shoes on."

He was highly impressed when I conformed and delighted when I addressed him as chief. He had achieved the rank of Chief Petty Officer Stoker in the Navy. He most certainly had a service mentality.

"All ranks above me are gods and those underneath me are shit."

He told me frequently that this way of conducting affairs was also correct in the business world. McDaid was happy that managers and foremen had their own toilets and locker rooms. I think he was convinced that the peerage had blue blood. This hierarchal or caste system lasted well in to the sixties.

AGNES GLYNN

Hair stood on the back of my neck when Agnes Glynn sang. Noisy drinkers grew silent in the public bar, service was halted, the tills stopped and Maria Barnes rested her ample bosom on the bar. Even Sam the Eel stubbed out his cigar and paused, whiskey glass half way to his lips. All the expectancy before a great performance. Agnes came alive on Monday nights. With Countess Heggar playing the piano, the rapt and dreamy look on Agnes' face transported us to another place. The shabby old bar in W10 became a wonderland. Without the aid of microphone or amplifier she sang songs from her native land.

Normally a gentle and reserved lady, she blossomed when she sang. *Moore's Melodies*, *Genevieve* and *Danny Boy* were delivered with great feeling. Sam the Eel invariably dabbed his eyes with a large white handkerchief on those evenings. She always finished her recital with the *Old Rugged Cross* and the applause would not have been out of place in the Albert Hall.

I felt sad on those evenings. I think I felt it was a shame that this great talent would never be heard outside of the King's and her local church. She often said, "God has given me a voice and I try to thank him in the church choir on Sunday mornings."

This stout, plainly dressed woman was highly thought of in W10. Even her fellow landladies tried to curb their worst excesses in her presence. Sam the Eel called her the Reverend Mother and when he heard that one of her lodgers had absconded with six weeks rent, he took immediate action. Handing her twenty pounds and a bunch of flowers one evening, he said, "Jimmy apologises for the delay."

Agnes smiled and said, "People are so good." Sam neglected to tell her that one of his friends had twisted Jimmy's arms so far behind his back that it just left him room to extract twenty pounds from his hip pocket.

Agnes Glynn came from a poor family in Dublin. She was an only child. When she was two, her mother descended into the depths of madness and died in an asylum. Her father opted out and left her with his mother, he then vanished out of her life. Her granny died when she was four. Then it was an orphanage run by nuns; she never spoke of her years there. She entered service at fifteen, a general dogsbody for a large family in Kildare. She dreamed that one day her absent father would come back.

He never did, but when she was eighteen she decided to track him down. She went to England as a student nurse and contacted the Salvation Army. They located him in Westbourne Park, where he had made a new life and ran a lodging house with his new wife. She wrote to him. It was not an angry or judgemental letter and the upshot was a tearful reunion. His new wife welcomed her and she moved into their home.

This sweet natured woman cared for them when they got old and nursed her father through a long illness until he died. She inherited the house and a little money and with hard work made a successful business. Despite a busy life she made time to sing in the choir on Sundays and in the King's on Mondays. She also made time to keep a fresh supply of fresh flowers on the altar of her local church.

I did some work for her. I noticed how different her flat was. It had a monastic simplicity and she told me that at one time she had toyed with the idea of joining a religious order. The floor was of well sanded pine wood with a rich dark varnish at the edges. The walls and ceiling were white and a dark wooden crucifix hung in the centre of a breast piece. The fireplaces were polished until they gleamed. There was a coffee table in the centre of the room; it just held her prayer book and rosary beads.

I felt I should keep the noise to a minimum. I was inclined to speak in whispers as Agnes Glynn moved around her domain with all the modesty and downcast eyes of a young novitiate. How different to Monday nights, then she would come alive. I could then listen to her beautiful voice and pick up the emotion, regret and perhaps the frustration in her songs. Was she happy? Difficult to know. She was certainly liked by all who knew her, this complex woman, with the angelic look on her face when she sang.

SAM THE EEL

"I saw my first sunrise through the spokes of the caravan wheels, Patrick, all horse drawn in those days." Sam the Eel sipped from his whiskey glass and sighed reflectively. "I have been in every town in the United Kingdom and Ireland; I have worked on every race track in the country at one time or another."

I was seventeen and I looked up to Sam; cauliflower ears and a nose splayed across his face, told of many defeats in the ring but there was an air about him. Camel hair overcoat, well cut suits and highly polished shoes were symbols of success to me.

"Never deny your roots Patrick; this town is full of two pint howlers and weekend millionaires. Respect people but never be overawed by them; we all bleed when we are cut."

Sam got a good living as a street bookmaker and his mother told fortunes by appointment. They lived in Westbourne Grove and I became quite friendly with the family when I repaired a brass tripod for Sam's mother, Rachael.

When I returned the tripod I discovered she kept her crystal ball on it. She showed me her tarot cards and treasured glass figurines. She was a swarthy woman of medium size, with a face wrinkled like a prune. Her hair was jet black, swept up and kept in place by a red bandana. She had three rings on each finger including her thumbs. The floor was covered with beautiful rugs and the walls were awash with beautiful mirrors and bunches of feathers from the most exotic of birds. The crystal ball was kept discreetly behind a curtain in the alcove and it was here that hopeful customers were shown glimpses of the future.

"Patrick, you will have a drink with me, and I owe you some silver." She poured whiskey into tumblers and began to speak of the old days, "I miss the open roads Patrick, but Sam was getting old and we had to settle. It's warmer and we have more room here, its cushti."

I refused payment for my work on the tripod.

"I never take money from widows or orphans and I always wish that the silver I leave behind will be the beginning of their riches".

She laughed uproariously and said a few words in Romany. "You know your people, Patrick." She gave me a gypsy blessing and when I left said, "You will never be rich but you'll never go short." Life has proved her correct.

When Sam was fourteen his parents felt he should contribute to the family finances. His father, Jim, was boxing nightly and Rachael told fortunes. Sam was given four swing boats as his fortune. When he had learnt to erect and operate those, he just had to collect the sixpences and stop the boats when the swinger's time ran out. This was achieved by raising a plank which brought the boats to a halt. During busy weekends he took a lot of sixpences and when he was fifteen he hired another young Romany and bought a roulette wheel. Even though bets were for pennies, the turnover was fast and furious and Sam without the benefit of schooling learnt to calculate the odds.

"I soon learnt that people want a lot for a little, Patrick," he told me. His father stood in the boxing booth nightly and paid a pound, if opponents went five minutes with him in the ring.

Sam was very proud that by eighteen he owned two horses and his own caravan. He had also learnt to read and write and arithmetic was second nature to him. His parents were delighted and felt it was time they had grandchildren. Word was sent out to numerous families. Sam was not terribly keen.

"I've had plenty of female company Patrick."

Rachael was scandalised when a few didicoy girls came to answer their publicity drive. She gave them the Romany language test and none of them were cushti.

On the first week of June, Romanies from the four corners gathered on Epsom Downs. It was Derby week and the highlight of the Romany year. Horse trading and matchmaking went on around the clock. Large camp fires glowed at night and violins played the haunting melodies of the travelling tribes.

Somehow Sam escaped the bands of matrimony. Some families feared Jim; he had a reputation as a pugilist and Rachael insisted on large dowries. Sam the Eel was too slippery for the constraints of a wedding. Continuously on the move and mobile phones not yet invented he remained single and his loving mother fussed over him all the more.

About this time Jim had begun to lose the occasional fight. It was time Sam learnt the rudiments of the noble art. Every morning he boxed three rounds with his dad and was gradually introduced to the business. He began to show promise and the fraternity watched with interest as he won a few amateur fights. He employed another young fellow to look after his swing boats.

"My business was all cash, Patrick, and I had to have honesty and loyalty."

These traits are difficult to get hold of but Sam's interviews were simple, "If you rob me you'll have no need to fear the police but I will be terribly, terribly disappointed."

He was lucky in his choices and both his lads were helped by Sam in later life to buy dodgem cars and a rifle range. In his own words, "Patrick, it's the poor that helps the poor."

Sam turned professional and his mother did not like what she saw in her crystal ball. He left the fairgrounds and took a flat in Notting Hill Gate. He got a manager and began to train seriously. He won a couple of fights and was amazed at the expenses incurred in the game. Superbly fit and supremely confident he began pushing his manager to get him into the big time. He won some fights in Lime Grove, always against Americans who had not quite made it on the Yankee circuit. However he was getting known and was matched against a Canadian light weight. He lost every round and got knocked out in the eighth. I think his ego suffered

"I felt I was King, Patrick, and this young kid put me on the floor."

After that Sam was always at the bottom half of the bill. He won a few but lost a lot and his handsome features were rearranged all over his face. Fairgrounds were losing their popularity, Hitler was getting restless in Europe and Sam was floating around on the fringes of gangland. When war broke out Sam was bouncing in the West End spielers,

"I should have listened to my mother Patrick, when she read my horoscope."

When Hitler got serious Sam joined the Merchant Navy. Jim had grown too old for the boxing ring and Rachael told fortunes in all the south coast seaside towns.

The days of the open road had drawn to a close and they lived in a succession of seaside boarding houses. It broke Jim's heart and he died before the end of the war. His caravan was locked up and under the arches in Shepherds bush.

After his death, Sam who was on shore leave took his mother to an open space in Ruislip and they burned his caravan. A fellow Romany had towed it to the site. Sam's eyes filled with tears recalling, "It was a moonlit night, the flames shot up, mother threw Dad's ashes onto the fire and then we were surrounded by half the Thames Valley police force."

Sam talked himself out of trouble, explaining to a sympathetic policeman the importance of the ritual to his mother. The Eel slipped away and avoided prosecution.

He bore a charmed life, torpedoed twice he was picked up by friendly ships on both occasions. When the war ended he swallowed the anchor and joined his mother in Brighton. She was scratching a living telling fortunes on the pier and Sam's business had long ago passed into other hands. The Eel fell in love with a Dutch Wall of Death rider. He married quickly to his mother's disgust and tried his hand at all in wrestling. He traded horses along the south coast, tic-tacked at the race tracks and was forced to act as doorman in some of the south coast spielers. His young wife became disenchanted with his lack of success in the money making business and left him for a diamond merchant.

When Rachael's daughter-in-law vanished for pastures new, she surprised Sam by telling him she had enough silver to buy a flat in Westbourne Grove. She still told fortunes but only by appointment. Sam working under the auspices of the race track gangs began a bookmaking business. Most of the local landladies liked a bet and with Sam's mother helping them to see into the future, mother and son prospered and were accepted as friends.

The Harrow Road was Sam's fiefdom, always skating on thin ice, never completely at ease with the law, this lovable rogue was aptly named Sam the Eel.

PETER JONES

"I come from the valleys boyo, educated in the university of life and from a race that's helped to civilise the world." Peter Jones, chair of philosophy or at least the high stool in the King's. "We gave you rugby, choirs and lardy cake; we sent St Patrick to take Christianity to the Irish; we have a nation of poets, singers and dreamers." There was always some wag to point out that they also had miners all over London without a colliery in sight.

Peter's early days in W10 were spent mixing with saloon bar society. He was tall, handsome and nicely dressed, articulate and courteous and with a pleasant singing voice. He had an air of mystery and in his cups hinted at unrequited love back in the Rhondda. "Listen boyo, whiskey is not as sweet as a woman's lips but it's a damn sight more sincere."

With coal dust ingrained in his skin and the iron deep in his soul, he carried some deep hurt like an albatross on his back. He hated the system that demanded men to crawl on their bellies in the bowels of the earth and to die, in many cases, gasping for breath.

Peter was not the type to fight the system; he jacked his job in and went to live with an aunt in Cardiff. She had a little money and for a time was glad of the company. She eventually threw him out as he made no attempt to get a job and spent his small savings in the Jolly Shepherd.

Customers in Burtons Menswear were always given tea and two rich tea biscuits. One Saturday morning Peter sipped tea ate his two biscuits and ordered the best of everything in the shop. The manager was on a bonus. When individual sales exceeded ten pounds. Peter walked out of Burtons looking like a million dollars. The total had come to ten pounds and ten shillings. He had paid three pounds and the tally man would collect the rest with interest.

"It was quite common boyo, a shilling a week and never at home."

Peter left on the night train for Paddington and became one of many question marks on the tally man's book.

Peter's arrival in W10 went unnoticed. He had two pounds which left him few options. Scrumpy was sixpence a glass so he found himself in Conner's Cider House. Mr McPhee was a valued customer here and he also managed a flop house for an absent landlord. Peter explained his position and was granted shelter for the night.

It was a dreadful place, full of rising damp, and the smell of stale fish, and boiled cabbage assailed the nostrils at all times. Conditions forced Peter to get a job and move to a place where he could hang up his good suit. It was not an executive position and he had to borrow some working clothes to carry the hod on a muddy building site.

Going from mining to the building trade is jumping from the frying pan into the fire and Peter soon discovered that sand and cement under your fingernails is just as unpleasant as coal dust. He was soon off with a bad back, and anyhow, he liked to dress smartly. He resigned from the building industry. Having spent a lot of time polishing saloon bar counters from the wrong end, he felt he was suited to the licensing trade. Being articulate and of smart appearance he got a job as barman in the Queen's Arms and was flavour of the month with his new employees.

Despite many offers he studiously avoided contact with the fairer sex. Now living over the pub he lived quite happily and was promoted to head barman. Arthur and Aida, the licensees, left him to run the place as they were near retirement. Most of the clientele were Welsh and it became known as the Cardiff Arms.

In 1939 Peter had no wish to fight the Germans, "I was given no option boyo, conscripted with minimum training and then on to a troop ship and found myself fighting Rommel in the desert."

Unlike a lot of the desert rats he never mentioned his part in the German leader's downfall. Wearing his demob suit he was back on the Harrow Road in 1945 and was given his old job in the Queen's Arms. Arthur and Aida were now very old and were glad to see him back.

Things were not back to normal as Peter's drinking had spiralled out of control. He functioned after a fashion, and being popular, people closed their eyes to his lapses. Arthur and Aida were on a cruise and he failed to open at eleven one morning. This coincided with a visit from an ambitious regional manager. Peter was eventually woken from a drunken sleep in the cellar and was given one hour to get off the premises.

Sam the Eel resplendent in Saville Row suit, camel hair overcoat and patent leather shoes gazed admiringly at his white cuffs and gold cufflinks; a crisp copy of *The Sporting Life*, open at yesterday's results on the table at his elbow. Peter Jones, homeless, jobless and depressed dropped his holdall and slumped down at the next table.

"Off on holiday then Peter?"

Peter gazed into space,

"Large whiskey and a pint for Peter, please Maria."

Peter nodded his thanks and silence descended. Sam looked at his well- manicured fingertips and realised that Peter was in some sort of trouble.

Four whiskeys later Peter, now relaxed in the womb of the King's, told Sam of his fall from grace. Sam listened, nodding his head sagely. Frequent visits from Sam's runners punctuated Peter's confessions. As he watched in wonder, betting slips and money disappeared into Sam's inside pocket. The Eel and his squad of runners were well known on the Harrow Road. It was all illegal but the police did not worry Sam, he always contributed to the Widows and Orphans Fund, and in fact some of them were his customers.

Before the end of the drinking session Peter had been recruited into Sam's squad. The Eel promised he would teach him the business and the rudiments of tic-tac and introduce him to the faces on the race track. The Eel assured him it was a wonderful career move. His new job enabled Peter to visit all the pubs on the Harrow Road daily. Being a bagman for Sam the Eel was very lucrative, so collecting bets and sampling the ale in each pub became a way of life for Peter.

Street bookmaking was heavily dependent on three things. You had to be trusted by the punters; you had to be at collection points on time, and you had to have enough money to pay without question when a customer had a big win. Peter's heavy drinking was not conducive to good time-keeping and his lapses caused the Eel a lot of anguish. Sam tried to help him but in the end had to sack him and use his considerable charm to save him from a beating from angry customers.

Despite the fact that Peter was liked by most people he never again held a full time job. Big functions and proprietors desperate for barmen occasionally gave him a little bit of money for the cider house and he became a general dogsbody and pot man at the Duke of Kent. He stumbled on from one crisis to the next until one fateful evening he met Molly Ryan, twice divorced and roaming the Harrow Road on a manhunt.

MRS JONES

Blue veins were beginning to radiate around her nose. Despite classical high cheek bones, her cheeks were bloated with a boozer's purple tinge. Her dressing gown, once white, was spotted with cigarette burns. Her blonde grey hair, showing traces of smoke staining, was plastered across her perspiring forehead. When she had answered the door, after a long period of banging on the big brass knocker, her feet were encased in furry slippers. She did not lift her feet as she shuffled along. With a thickening waist and nicotine stained fingers she bore no resemblance to the slim, attractive girl gazing adoringly at a merchant navy officer in the wedding photo on the wall.

Time had dealt harshly with Mrs Jones. A half empty whiskey bottle had pride of place on the dining room table. Surrounded by several empty beer bottles and two overflowing ash trays, the overpowering smell of stale beer was everywhere. It was Sunday, mid-morning on a depressing rain soaked day in early September. I waited patiently for an inch of fag ash to drop off the end of Molly's cigarette.

"There is nothing wrong with your heating, Mrs Jones."

"Why have I no heating or hot water this morning?"

"Your fire has gone out, I just lit it. You need to put two buckets of coal and bank the fire each night."

I was wasting my breath. Most evenings Molly was seeing double and stoking a boiler was low on her agenda.

Only when unscrupulous plumbers began billing her for work when they had just re-lit the fire did she confide in her friend Mrs Doyle. I was sent to check and had to tell her the problem was of her own making. A grown woman, she acted like a child that had been told off, and apologised for her forgetfulness.

"I cannot offer you tea Patrick, that frigging milkman is late again." I decided not to remind her that she had called him a lazy fucker and dispensed with his services the previous night.

"Do you miss your home and family?"

I told her that occasionally I did. She poured out two large whiskeys, the bottle playing a tattoo on the rim of the glasses. She slumped into an easy chair and with a sad faraway look in her eyes began to tell me about her childhood.

I had met Molly on several occasions with her Monday washday cronies. With her war paint on she scrubbed up quite well and I was unaware that she was on the skids. It was a revelation to listen to her life story up to the time she was divorced by Dennis Ryan. I listened with all the impatience of a young man but I was deeply moved by this sad woman as she tried to make sense of her chaotic lifestyle. Unfortunately I had not lived long enough to offer her any advice.

Molly Hayes was spoilt as a child. Her parents doted on her, and having some property they were able to indulge all her wishes. She was born in an Irish house in Paddington and being an only child her father gave her the idea that wanting something was three quarters of the way to getting it. Her whole world came crashing down when her father died when she was sixteen. She was to spend the remainder of her life trying to replace him. Unfortunately, there was no end of unscrupulous and predatory males willing to take advantage of her never ending search for love.

Molly's mother re-married and went to America leaving her daughter the owner of two large houses that would always guarantee her a good income. It would never compensate for the loneliness and feelings of loss. She embarked on a series of short lived torrid affairs and married a merchant seaman.

Chief Engineer Davis was thirty nine, a well-educated and gentlemanly chap, set in his ways and married to the sea. He was madly in love with Molly and all his leaves were periods of bliss. Loaded with presents from foreign ports, all his homecomings were welcomed like a new honeymoon.

Absence makes the heart grow fonder; of course it is also said, out of sight out of mind, and Molly a young woman with healthy appetites missed Ron from her bed forty weeks out of fifty two. She sought the company of her peers in the saloon bar of the King's. Alcohol blurs the raw edges of loneliness and soon she found friends of her own age group. The companionship and fun helped to while away the long evenings but it was never enough. With Ron her husband, father figure and lover sailing over the blue, she found comfort in the arms of a randy barrow boy in his fifties. She soon dumped him for a policeman close to retiring age and then moved on to the window cleaner who was quite advanced for his age, and only did the windows at street level as he had no head for heights.

Affairs conducted on the Harrow Road had a tendency to become common knowledge and Ron Davies had relatives in the area. Despite the fact that they were rather superior people and had shunned public houses, they soon got wind of the Jezebel that had joined their family. They informed Ron, who set a trap. The sailor home from the sea one early morning found Molly in the arms of the baker.

Chief Engineer Davis was a civilised man. He gazed at a copy of the *Kama Sutra* whilst the baker got dressed. He calmly returned the lover's guide to the bedside table, packed his few possessions and despite Molly's tears walked out of her life. Divorce followed quickly and Molly, her reputation now in tatters, found herself seeking love even more desperately.

Men floated in and out of her life and quite a few took advantage of her generosity. She was a sucker for a plausible tale and her need for male company made her vulnerable. She lent money to no-hopers and long distance kids, and as most of her lovers were older men she spent a lot of time visiting them in hospital. She was single for about a decade when Dennis Ryan came to lodge in one of her houses. He was not as old as she would have liked but by that time she was sick of other women's husbands and wanted one of her own.

Dennis Ryan was a bricklayer. A hard working man of sober habits, he was forty-four when a big job brought him to W10. Brought up in an orphanage in Ireland, he had learnt a trade and had worked all over the country. He was a loner by nature, but when he came to lodge in Molly's house he was fascinated by this fast, liberated woman. He chased her until she caught him. They bought a flat and Dennis was thrilled by the first real home he had ever had. He treated his wife like a lady. Molly's friends noticed that she calmed down for a while and seemed content to play the dutiful wife.

Despite her demons she tried to make a go of her marriage. She strayed from time to time but Dennis closed his eyes to it. Then she began to treat him in an off-hand manner and to flirt outrageously with older men, especially when they were out together. Mrs Doyle said that was the time he should have put her across his knee. I have always doubted that that would have worked. Molly being of a perverse nature and having read the *Kama Sutra* from cover to cover would have more than likely relished the antics. Instead Dennis behaved like a rabbit dazzled by the headlights.

Dennis worked a seven day week during the war. He had been just too old for call up and was always in demand because of war damage. He began to move about the country once more and the marriage fell apart. His visits home now infrequent, the marriage dragged on until 1951 when Dennis met a nurse from a local hospital. He packed, left and divorced Molly in 1951. She never saw him again.

Molly was now losing her looks, drinking heavily, and comfort eating and growing ever more desperate. Her circle of friends became very judgemental and over protective of their men. Words like 'whore' and 'nymphomaniac' were bandied about. She became a source of gossip among her peers. Mrs Doyle was the one honourable exception who tried to reach out to this unhappy woman. Being a divorced woman herself, she empathised with many of her problems and eventually using tea and sympathy and friendship managed to stabilise her a little. Somehow or other Molly came to the conclusion that a young man for some robust love making would be the answer to her dilemma.

It worked for a number of years; Jimmy a twenty-five year old barrow boy became her lover. She rewarded him with good suits, watches and rings. Martin, who was a well- known queen, became her friend and confidant. He visited her at eleven most mornings and they grew quite close. He advised her on fashion and skin creams and how she should wear her hair. He became very important to her and when he died suddenly she was devastated.

With Martin dead, Molly began to drink heavily at lunch time. The Monday ritual with the rest of the landladies of W10 was no longer enough. She let herself go to the extent that court appearances were frequent. She had plenty of money but her demons began to drag her down. She had no need to frequent the cider house, but one night on automatic pilot, she staggered in to Conner's. Peter Jones was in earnest conversation with Jack the Wobbly when Molly placed her well upholstered posterior on the adjacent seat. She made her selection quickly and as Jack got up and walked out, he had no idea that this boy from the valleys would be her next husband.

THE BESPOKE SUIT

I cannot really explain why I felt that I needed a really expensive suit the week I joined the Communist Party. When I told Sam the Eel about the suit he said I was just having an attack of middle class aspirations. Then Jock McLaren told me that joining the party was a bad career move. I had been invited to a cousin's wedding and with the foolishness of youth I felt it might impress relatives. I kept reading the Marxist pamphlets; they stated that I had nothing to lose but my chains, so why the hell did I want an expensive suit?

Mr Green was barely five feet tall. He had a bald, shiny head and an expressive face. He had twinkling, humorous eyes and wore gold horn rimmed glasses. He was always immaculately dressed; a well-cut three-piece suit and a pocket watch on a gold chain proudly displayed across his waistcoat. His front teeth were gold-capped and along with a huge gold bracelet on his wrist, he had gold rings on the fourth finger of each hand. Standing in front of his tailor's shop, on the Harrow Road, he seemed to glitter when the sun shone. He was a generous man and gave freely to local charities. He also made top quality suits for hundreds of well-heeled clients.

The sign over the door said Isodore Green Master Tailor. The window showed just one well-cut suit and stated prices from fifteen guineas. The shop had a beautiful, mahogany entrance door and the window was of Georgian plate glass. It looked the business at a time when Burtons could clothe the masses for five pounds and even throw in a waistcoat and tie. Isodore's customers wanted something extra and they got it. He was proud of his membership of the Master Tailor's Guild and all clients were treated like royalty.

Daily he drove to his business from his home in Golders Green. He picked up his friend and employee on route. Abe was a wizened, silent little man who sat cross-legged on his work bench at the back of the shop. He finished off the suits with the skill and patience of generations. He had numbers tattooed close to his left wrist and he kept a blue and white flag on his bench: blue and white the colour of the Tallit, the prayer shawl that never left his side. He was like Isodore, a native of Plonsk, a little town thirty-five miles from Warsaw. Both men were well known and respected by the Jewish community, and Isodore looked after Abe as if he was family.

I replaced a defective heater for Isodore. When he paid me. I told him I would like to buy one of his suits and that I had the necessary fifteen guineas. He looked at me sadly. "Patrick, my boy, fifteen guineas is the bottom of my range and would severely restrict your choice."

Fifteen guineas was a month's wages for me and I realised that apprentices were not numbered amongst Isodore's clientele. I left the shop slightly depressed and went to talk to my mentor, Sam the Eel. He pointed out that champagne tastes and lemonade money were a poor combination. He went on a bit and told me that man's richness was in the fewness of his needs. I was not fully convinced and asked why he never shopped at Burtons. He chuckled, patted me on the back, lit a cigar and ordered another whiskey. I still wanted a bespoke suit but by now it was getting to be an obsession.

Mr Green drank in the King's occasionally, and one day I asked him what his opinion of the suit I was wearing was. He looked at me kindly and answered, "Patrick, I shall tell you the truth; it's a pawk; a suit it is not, already."

I agreed and told him I could now afford twenty pounds. He lit a cigar and prepared to lecture.

"Put your money in the bank Patrick; who do you need to impress? You will hardly ever wear it and it will hang in a dusty wardrobe. I would hate to take your money, you're a hard working boy, and I speak to you as if you were my own son."

I had a lot of respect for Mr Green but I was still fascinated with the well-cut suit in his window.

Next day I met him on the street, he was on his way to the bank but he stopped to talk. "Patrick, do not get taken in by the people who buy my suits. They need to impress; they have a position to uphold. Quite a few need to borrow money, and you never attempt that wearing a shabby suit."

I gazed through Mr Green's shop window at least twice a week and I went to party meetings once a week. A stunning looking girl from Derry had joined the party; she was eighteen and so different from the ladies I knew. We frequently discussed how we were going to change the system. She was a student nurse and neither drank nor smoked. I knew an expensive suit would not impress Shelia as she stood at railway stations and sold the *Daily Worker* on her day off. We became close and I got the impression she wanted our relationship to move on from platonic. However I had problems with that. I still looked forward to party meeting nights and being invited to the nurse's home in Maida Vale. She differed from me enormously, as the iron was deep in her soul. Shelia had seen the worst facets of poverty and tribalism in her native city and was committed to change. I was aware that I did not have the integrity or enough fire in my belly. We both studiously read Karl Marx and he did state that all profit was theft, so why the hell was I still hankering after a bespoke suit?

Mr Green called me to his shop one day. "You really got your heart set on a good suit, already."

I told him that I now had thirty pounds.

"Put it in the bank, Patrick, maybe we can work something out."

He took a catalogue from his pocket and showed me a state of the art Parkway glass fronted fire and back boiler."

"Can you install one of these, Patrick?"

I assured him that I could but that it would mean a week's work and a lot of mess and no hot water for a week. He told me that Harvey, his wife, was going to Israel for a month and he would like the work carried out in her absence.

We ordered the boiler that day and I arranged a week's holiday at work. I told him that to save travelling time I would like to move into his house in Golders Green, as that could insure I worked late if required. He was impressed and agreed readily, as he was going to stay at his sister's in Finchley. I trusted him especially when he pointed out that one of his suits should have the right accessories,

"A good shirt, cufflinks, a silk tie and good leather shoes are a must, my boy."

I pointed out that my money would not stretch that far.

"Patrick, we have a saying in the old country, what costs no money, can't be dear."

I moved into his house, and twelve hours into the job I realised I had under-estimated the time it would take. Living on fish and chips, drinking lots of coffee and working eighteen hour days, I finished on time. It looked a picture and with all the services restored I got some paint from the garage to touch up any damage.

Mr Green and half the congregation of the local synagogue came to see the finished job. Sometime in the evening I was dropped back to Westbourne Park. I was drunk, exhausted and had lost eight pounds weight over the week. There was a great sense of satisfaction with a job well done. I had been introduced to car dealers, import and export merchants, jewellers and the local rabbi. I had a dozen business cards in my pocket and enough promises to make me a millionaire. I had seen another way of life but my mind was in turmoil. Shelia would be disappointed I had missed the party meeting and what she thought was becoming very important to me. Did I have any integrity? Should I stifle my ambition and join her selling the *Daily Worker*? Was I too deeply committed to an affair going nowhere? Was I capable of deceit? Could I have one erotic affair and still have a heady romance? Why was I still obsessed with a bespoke suit? Was it all about passion, warmth, tousled hair on pillows and the beautiful scent of a woman? Was that the real meaning of life?

Mr Green took some measurements shortly after that. I thought he winced a little when I choose material from the top of his range; it was blue with a chalk stripe. I told him my shoe size and his friend, Mr Glickstein, came to the shop with a beautiful pair of leather shoes. Harvey, his wife, had sent me two lovely shirts and a letter of thanks. Her cousin, Mr Gosla, had left a gold snake ring, which just fitted my little finger. I had to return for a second fitting and I really thought that when I wore it, it would be the best day of my life.

The following Saturday I made my grand entrance to the King's saloon bar. I had been to the barber shop and I felt really good in my regalia and then I had no clear idea who I wished to impress. With hand stitched lapels, hand-made shirt, silk tie, snake ring and shoes that shone, I was starting to get the confidence that comes with nice possessions. The bar had just one customer at that early hour. Peter Jones was gazing into an empty whiskey glass and the barman was engrossed in the *Sporting Life*. I got two whiskeys and sat next to Peter. He thanked me and said, "Have you robbed a bank boyo? You look like a cross between a Philadelphia lawyer and a pox doctor's clerk."

I next called to see Isodore and Abe. They praised the suit and made me a cup of coffee. When I left the shop Isodore gave me six camphor balls. "Patrick, my boy, it's a picture; fits like the paper on the wall, but it's just for weddings, funerals and bar mitzvahs."

Kathleen and Dot Dunne were having a midday snack when I called. Kathleen said it looked classy and lovingly stroked my silk tie, and then Dot said, "It has probably cost more than I have spent on clothes in my lifetime," looking at Kathleen sourly.

My next call was to Shelia in Maida Vale. The bus conductor asked if my limousine had broken down and Shelia never noticed anything for half an hour as her nose was stuck in a large volume of Mark and Engels. When she finally noticed she lectured me on the sweat shops in the rag trade, gave me a peck on the cheek and rushed off to pick up the afternoon shift at the hospital.

I returned to the King's, where Sam the Eel immediately asked me if I had had a legacy. He really enjoyed it when I told him it had come about as the result of the barter system. He felt it appropriate that I should have a large glass of whiskey and a cigar whilst he examined the ‘smutter’, as he called it. Maria Barnes with a real effort at massaging my ego said she wished she was thirty years younger.

All this sartorial elegance brought nothing new to my life, so I went sadly back to my lodgings. After carefully putting camphor balls in each pocket I hung the bespoke suit in a dusty old wardrobe. Takes more than a good suit to change a lifestyle. Uncle had been right when he said, “A man without learning and wearing fine clothes is like a gold ring on a barrow pig’s nose.”

W10 FUNERAL

When Peter Jones left the valleys, never in his wildest dreams had he aspired to being driven in a beautiful coach drawn by two high-stepping horses, all complete with a driver in top hat and driving gloves. Shame he had to die to achieve it.

Rain bucketed down as Peter's funeral made its way along the Harrow Road. Most of the corner shops, being owned by Welshmen, had their blinds drawn. Peter the pot man certainly got respect on his last journey to Kensal Rise.

It was an impressive cortege, with the horses black plumes and the Daimler Bentleys which brought the traffic to a standstill. The journey from the marital home took only twenty minutes.

Peter was not a great believer, but Molly, his widow, had two clergymen at the graveside. It was a nice service and the widow shed a few obligatory tears

"We just had six months together but I know he died happy."

This was debatable. When they married she made him pack his job in and he had taken to frequenting Conner's Cider House in Penn Street. He had told some of his cronies there that things were far from idyllic.

"I am not the marrying type, I was low in funds and Molly Ryan can be very persuasive. Her two previous husbands walked away and I can understand it, the woman is insatiable. Every night, and I with the heavy sleep of the cider on me, she places her freezing arse in my lap and makes sure she wakes me up. Is that any way to treat a man of sixty?"

The bedroom shenanigans must have told on him. One evening after five pints of scrumpy he suffered a massive heart attack. Most of his cronies were spaced out and never noticed until the landlord found him at closing time. Cider drinkers have very red faces, so it is understandable.

We waited until the grave was filled in and Molly in her widow's weeds perked up. She gazed lustfully at one of the pallbearers and invited him back to the King's for refreshments. The poor man was scandalised and explained that he had to return to his family immediately.

Glad to leave the windswept graveyard, we piled into the limousines and returned to the blazing fire and a huge buffet at the King's. Maria, the landlady, had excelled herself and greeted the mourners with large glasses of whiskey, rum or gin. The newly widowed Molly Jones gave a little speech.

"Peter would have loved to see you all here; he would have loved to see the horses as he always liked a bet."

We raised our glasses to the absent one and as people seldom speak ill of the dead, Peter was soon elevated to sainthood.

Funeral teas can sometimes be sad, nostalgic or even fraught affairs. This one was none of these. What it was, was a very drunken party, or wake if you prefer. It was not pretentious; rationing had not quite finished but Maria had her sources and the buffet was superb. Smoked salmon and wide choices of wine were absent, but Maria stated in her no nonsense fashion, "There's three kinds of meat and for wine there's red, white and whiskey."

She had put the saloon out of bounds to the public. Two barmen kept occupied and no sound of the tills, the drinking was fast and furious. All the W10 ladies were dressed in their best dark outfits, all wearing big hats and of course their seal of office, the huge black handbags. It was Monday and to show respect to Mrs Jones they had all hired limousines and changed the habits of decades and cancelled the big wash. The consensus of opinion was that it would not kill the lodgers to sleep in the same sheets for a fortnight.

Rebecca Collins stayed close to Molly reminding her that she understood the heartache of losing a husband. "Every time I look at the banister I think of poor Luigi, and I curse that bastard Mussolini. He was responsible for Luigi's bad nerves.

When I married him he was half-starved and frightened. I put the weight back on him but he could not come to terms with his years in the POW camps. They all went funny in those camps, love; no female company you see.

"Luigi did some decorating for you Molly?"

"Oh, he did but I never got to talk to him, he was a good worker and ever so polite."

She stared quizzically at Rebecca and decided to circulate as she didn't like the way the conversation had turned and indeed he was one of the few men in the area she had not known in the biblical sense.

Widow Jones moved on to speak to Countess Heggar; she was greeted with a regal hug. The Countess was still in ladylike mode. Four gin and tonics later she would become Maggie Flynn from Waterford "You must be more careful love; Peter was number three wasn't he? Try to take more care of yourself," she said bitchily, eyeing Molly's nourished belly and spreading hips. "The late Count always said a woman should be careful of comfort eating," she remarked looking down at her own trim figure.

"Condescending old bitch," Molly muttered as she moved on.

Widow Jones next moved towards Joan Hayes. Joan was in a foul mood. "You are well shut of him love; look at that silly bastard I am lumbered with, a frigging waste of space. If I had my time over again I would avoid men like the plague. I'd get a tabby cat and a vibrator. But shure, it's useless talking to you Molly; you have always been man mad."

The grieving widow moved on deeply shocked by this outburst and Kathleen Doyle almost choked on a large gin and tonic.

Kathleen Doyle's friend Helena Brown and her husband travelled with us to the funeral and now Helena was beginning to lose her bearings and sway dangerously on her high heels. Her husband, Jack, seemed to get more miserable as the day wore on. He was a scrawny little man and he seemed dead scared of Helena. His Adam's apple bobbed up and down nervously as he saw Widow Jones make her unsteady way towards our table. Kathleen puffed nervously on a Craven A. Jack's shirt collar was several sizes too big for his neck and a thick coat of dandruff lay on his blue serge suit collar. Molly commenced to straighten Jack's tie and brush the white flakes from his collar. I really do not know if there was a history, but Helena bristled and told her to politely fuck off. Molly sashayed off into the crowd. Jack complained of extreme fatigue and left to walk home but not before Helena had told him to piss off, if he liked. I was not pleased with the turn of events as I could see me on escort duties later on, especially when Helena started tossing down large rums as if they were going out of fashion. Kathleen said that she would assist me in taking Helena home later. I suppose that in the valley of the blind the one-eyed man is king.

The wake had now been in progress for about eight hours and the noise was deafening, everybody talking and nobody listening. The widow felt it was time to liven up proceedings. Countess Heggar was playing the *Warsaw Concerto* and Agnes Glynn, encouraged by the grieving widow, was singing *When You Come Home Again to Wales*. Maria was serving tea and sandwiches in an attempt to sober up the crowd. The barmen gradually pulled the shutters down and the crowd began to scatter. I was young and had not drunk as much as many and so hailed cabs and helped to bring the wake to a close. Widow Jones had collapsed completely and had been put to bed upstairs but only after she had warned the barman to lock their doors. It was after midnight when Kathleen and I began escorting a now drunken Helena home.

Propping up a drunk on a foggy night in W10 is not one of life's great pleasures. I was getting quite hacked off with these duties as it had become the norm on Monday nights. Helena had become very noisy and had lost her inhibitions. "You know what she said to me when I went round to sympathise? 'The only way to get over a man is to get under another one'. Nothing young or old in trousers is safe with the black widow."

We had to stop frequently to listen to these pearls of wisdom.

"Did you see the performance with the pallbearer?"

Kathleen tried to hush her up as we were beginning to draw attention to ourselves. Ten yards from Harrow Road Police Station things took a turn for the worse. We were just unlucky that a well-dressed gentleman walked along the pavement taking his Chihuahua for a midnight stroll. Helena in her unsteady state leaned over to stroke the dog's head. The animal was highly strung and bit her finger. Helena fell over the dog's lead, and being quite a large woman pulled Kathleen and I to the ground. The dog went mad, his owner went berserk, a crowd gathered and Helena threw fucks at all and sundry.

Kathleen tried to retrieve the situation with a few calm words, apologising profusely to the dog's owner. Meanwhile I tried to lift Helena. This was impossible as the dog's lead was wrapped around her ankles. The dog was yapping furiously and then Helena passed out. The dog's owner became very precious and cast aspersions on the whole Irish race. Kathleen had a fiery nature and would not have her race denigrated; she gave him a slap and called him an Italian ponce. He went to hit her and I gave him a Glasgow kiss. His nose began to bleed and the assembled crowd began to bay for blood. In the ensuing pandemonium two policemen appeared as if by magic.

Someone had called an ambulance, Helena was whisked off to St. Mary's and Kathleen and I were invited to step into the station. She used all her diplomatic skills, but to no avail; she was taken home in a police car and I spent a night in the cells.

Due to Monday nights being quiet in the police station I had my own private cell. The desk sergeant told me that if it had been a Saturday I might have to share. All this with a sarcastic sneer, as he slammed the door. I had a hard bunk bed, two blankets and a large chamber pot. It had been a long day and I did not need any rocking. I got a mug of tea and a cold sausage sandwich at half past five. I was now sober and feeling sorry for myself. Kathleen left a clean set of clothes for me with the desk sergeant at half past six. Dot had advised her that a smart appearance was crucial at the magistrate's court. Dot knew these things as her husband was a career criminal.

Kathleen had also arranged a solicitor and was on her way to see the Italian dog owner.

As it turned out he was Turkish and I am convinced money was exchanged as he told the police, before the hearing, that he was not pressing charges. The magistrate gave me a long lecture and I must have looked suitably contrite. I was fined three guineas plus costs. Kathleen paid before we left the court. "It is the least I can do; you did step in when the ponce was about to lay it to me."

It was just nine days talk amongst the W10 ladies and then some fresher gossip came along. Helena was discharged from hospital, the dog owner wore dark glasses for a week and the widow Jones maintained that marrying and burying Peter had cost her a fortune. The even tempo of normality soon returned to the Harrow Road and life moved on.

THE BLACK PRINCE

The Black Prince was well known on the Harrow Road. Collecting non-ferrous metal only, he felt superior to the rest of the rag and bone fraternity. He loaded his scrap onto his bicycle trailer and took it to a dealer in Notting Hill Gate daily. He avoided the West Indians that were beginning to move into the area at the time. He used to say, "They are slaves and the sons of slaves; I am from Nigeria and of noble blood."

They in turn christened him the Black Prince. Six feet tall, well-built with dreadlocks and a beard, he looked quite a commanding figure. He was a man of set routines. He found morning ablutions unnecessary, as he slept in his clothes. His first port of call was Arthur and Aida's Café. They opened at six and gave him some sandwiches on condition that he dined al fresco. He ate those at the horse trough, washed down with water, and then commenced the business of the day. He pedalled his contraption through the streets calling at all small factories and private houses. When he was given some scrap, he thanked the donors and hoped that their tribes would increase. He always looked puzzled when his benefactors said, "I hope not." At the end of each day he called to a different lodging house and they always gave him a take away for his evening meal. He went back to his air raid shelter on a bomb site, made a fire in a brazier, lit an old oil lamp and settled down for the evening. I sometimes watched from my room, which overlooked the bomb site. He had no radio or reading material. What went through his mind as he sat there smoking and watching the flames?

He was visited by the authorities from time to time. The council had plans for the site and made copious notes about his lack of facilities. An ambitious vicar tried to get him to go to church. Various cults visited him to point out the error of his ways. They all left leaflets, which he used to light his fire. A very charming lady from the Salvation Army came around; she left quickly when he offered her a pinch of cannabis and told her she should indulge as it was the holy smoke. We all greeted him as 'Prince' and he always gave us a regal wave as he passed. In true princely fashion, with his stove pipe hat he had the freedom of Paddington.

Late one afternoon, surrounded by a crowd of jeering teenagers and pushing his contraption, he arrived at our workshop in Kensal Green. He came right into the workshop without a by your leave. We were very busy but Jock McLarren greeted him as if he was a valued customer. "To what do we owe the honour, Prince?"

The Prince answered quite formally, "I appear to have some mechanical trouble old boy; I need to speak to the Barra Sahib."

Jock puffed his turn-down pipe. "Prince, there is no need for Swahili here, I am the boss man."

The Prince inspected the workshop in his regal fashion and told the teenagers at the door to disperse. Jock, realising it was almost knocking off time called me over. "Patrick, see if you can help him; you will be late but I'll make it up to you."

The workshop emptied at five and I found myself working for the Black Prince. I did not consider it a great honour. He sat on one of the benches and made himself comfortable. The contraption was in a bad state. When I asked him to unload his trailer he said, "Young fellow, I have laboured in the heat of the day, my body now needs rest; you be thankful for your youth and strength.

"Did you know old chap that Prometheus is the God of fire?

I did but I guessed that despite now living in a bomb site the Black Prince had at some time had a classical education. When I had finished the Prince inspected everything and felt that it needed a coat of paint. "You must take pride in your work, young fellow."

I gave the trailer a coat of paint. "I hope this meets with your approval, Your Majesty. I just need your address to send the invoice."

He glared at me. "Please do not address me as 'Your Majesty', that title is reserved for my father; I am the second son of his number two wife. I will always be prince but never a king."

I apologised and made no further mention of an invoice. Shortly afterwards he gathered his bits and cycled up Kensal Green waving to his constituents.

The Prince did not work on Coronation Day. In fact he had spent the previous week making preparations. The students at Paddington Tech had made him a brass plaque 'By Appointment of Her Majesty the Queen'. They attached it to his trailer and told him that he should attend the Coronation. He was in complete agreement. He visited Paddington Baths for his annual wash, spent a couple of hours in the suds and then went to a barber he knew. The barber worked diligently getting the ashes out of his dreadlocks. He then trimmed and peroxided his beard. On leaving his shop, the barber, a staunch royalist, gave him a pound to toast the Queen's health. A Presbyterian minister gave him a long, black overcoat and a Catholic priest gave him brown boots and an Anthony Eden hat. Countess Heggar gave him a good quality shirt and cravat. He got a pair of brown gloves from Mrs Jones and also some socks belonging to one of her previous husbands.

He wore all this gear on the morning of the Coronation. It was not exactly colour coded but he still looked a striking figure.

He was advised to travel by tube on the big day, but putting his trust in some college students, he chose to ignore this. He left Westbourne Park at nine o'clock, having been told that if he was early he could sit with the VIPs at Westminster. The students observed the day events. He arrived at the Coronation route riding his contraption. He found it heavily policed. A kindly policeman told him that only heads of state were allowed past the cordon. Students from Paddington were close by and looking for excitement. They told the Prince that even lowly MPs were being let through. When he was told that the Queen of Tonga had been allocated three seats because of her bulk and that dignitaries from the West Indies were going through in dozens he flew into a rage. He retreated to some high ground and pedalling furiously downhill he tried to crash the barriers. Despite blood curdling war cries and cheers from the students, the Metropolitan Police stood firm. The Black Prince, his contraption and four students were taken to Saville Row Police Station.

I heard of the fiasco as I attended Paddington Tech on day release. I was told that on being released from police custody, the Prince had sold all his new regalia to Mick's Misfits on the Edgware Road and changed back into his decrepit old clothes. I met the Prince some time later and asked him how he had enjoyed the Coronation. He glared at me suspiciously and before pedalling off said "I was badly let down by the establishment, old boy."

The Black Prince died in a wheelbarrow, with the wheel resting against the wall and the handles on the ground. It had been his armchair and his bed. His bicycle and trailer were parked by his side. Cold ashes in his brazier and a darkened globe on his oil lamp showed he had been dead for some time. He had been born on the banks of the lordly Niger River but he had died with the sounds of the Paddington canal in his ears. Local boys had found him, sitting as if on a throne, clad in an old army overcoat, his tribal scars had long ago been covered with a straggly beard. His boots had seen better days and he never wore socks. Two tobacco tins completed his possessions; one was half full of Old Holborn the other contained a little bit of wacky baccy, or the 'holy smoke' as he used to call it.

Despite the best efforts of the authorities they were unable to trace any relatives. It looked as if the state would have to bury the Black Prince. After an inquest, the good-natured ladies of W10 decided that they would pay for his funeral. This was organised by Agnes Glynn and when some smart ass mentioned that he may have been a Muslim, she answered gently, "My father's house has many mansions."

She told me that I should attend the funeral. “It is one of the corporal works of mercy, Patrick, to bury the dead.”

Two cars were hired to follow the hearse and eight of us attended the burial. Agnes had asked the priest to come along and we had a little service at the graveside. So late one Saturday evening, far from the waving palm trees of Nigeria and under the stormy skies of Kensal Green, the Black Prince was laid to rest.

COUNTESS HEGGAR

I cannot say that we had conversations; she lectured and I listened. She was usually well lubricated when she imparted her gems of wisdom and as she lived only staggering distance from the pub, mercifully they were of short duration. Despite having to make sure she did not topple over, I can still recall a lot of what went on in the labyrinths of her mind.

She spoke frequently of her friends' lack of dress sense. "They slavishly follow every wave, and they waste their money on cheaply made rags. If only they would listen. Fashions change frequently, but style and class remain. Working class girls, Patrick, they haven't a clue."

I was sometimes tempted to ask her if she had descended from the peerage, but at eighteen I did not have the confidence to bring her back to earth. Stopping under a lamp post on one of my Monday night escort duties, she stated, "Good sex and plenty money are terribly important, but vulgar to speak about either."

I nodded in agreement; I knew she had plenty money but her sex life was shrouded in mystery.

The Countess learned to trust me and told me that she felt the Count would like her to remove the coal fire from her sitting room. I agreed to fit a modern gas fire, having told her this operation would take a full weekend. I commenced the work early one Saturday morning.

A large photograph of the dead Count stared haughtily down at me from above the mantel piece. She gazed adoringly at the handsome man. In his Polish officer's uniform and especially with his dress sword, I felt I was in the presence of greatness. I asked the Countess that in the interests of safety, if I could remove the picture from the breast piece.

Drawing herself to her full height she informed me that on no account could the Count be moved. The dust sheets were down and a gleaming new fire awaited fitting. I pleaded with her, explained that I had to use tools and that the Count risked being covered with soot or worse still being knocked to the floor. She was adamant and burst into tears. I clumsily tried to comfort her and told her we could cancel the whole operation, if she so wished. Gradually she stopped crying and calmed down.

She poured us two large whiskeys and began to tell me of her life. She did not mention her youth in Ireland. Her eyes sparkled as she spoke of musical evenings and dinner parties with wall to wall Polish officers, after the war, in Maida Vale. The Count, with all the social graces: the romantic courtship, marriage at Brompton Oratory, honeymoon in Rome, audience with the pope and a special blessing, the ocean cruise to America, then visiting all his rich and powerful cousins. Even though the Count had lost his vast estates in Poland, he had sufficient money to buy two large houses, and a nice private flat as the marital home. The Count's hardships gave her a great hatred of fascists and communists and also made her a card carrying member of the Conservative Party.

I listened respectfully to tales of the married years, the Count's ability to make money on the Stock Exchange, the travel, the parties, good wine and restaurants. It seemed a truly hedonistic lifestyle. She mentioned that children never came along but as they were so much in love they never missed them. Her voice cracking with emotion she described the Count's death from cancer at fifty.

Maggie Flynn, known as Countess, made up for her lack of inches by staring down her nose at all and sundry. Peter Jones said that small people had to sniff a lot of armpits and this sometimes gave them a disdainful look. Never the less she was very attractive, in a petite sort of way, well proportioned, pointed bosom and a good pair of legs. With a good sense of dress, she was the queen bee amongst the W10 ladies. With three staff all ready to jump through hoops for her, she had no need to take part in the everyday running of her boarding houses, but she did like to join the other ladies at the Monday ritual in the bag wash.

Despite our backgrounds being similar she seldom spoke of her youth in Ireland. I gather she had left at fifteen and went to work as a children's nanny for an American family in Maida Vale. They had treated her well and encouraged her to play the piano. She showed remarkable aptitude and was soon treated as one of the family. Invited to all family social occasions, it was probably about that time that she became superior and began to act in a grander fashion than her employers. Elocution lessons followed and she became quite the sophisticate. The American family being of Polish extraction kept open house for lots of glamorous Polish pilots that were everywhere at the end of the war.

Sitting on the high stool at the King's and surrounded by her acolytes, she believed in her superiority. She had travelled extensively, she dressed well, and she had flown in an aeroplane when her companions had none of these experiences. She had been married and widowed and not a breath of scandal surrounded her name. A polish butcher had attempted to kiss her hand once but one of her haughty looks froze the very marrow in his bones. In his broken English he explained to his friends, "Countess, she will not make music with butcher, she needs a duke at least to light her fire."

A Ukrainian gentleman brought flowers to one of her birthday parties. She rebuffed him in the nicest possible way. Explaining that flowers gave her hay fever and sneezing very daintily into a small handkerchief, she asked the barman to put them in a vase in the back room. He clicked his heels, bowed to the Countess and vanished into the Harrow Road. Waving her cigarette holder, she explained to her friends, "He was a peasant, my dears, did you not see his finger nails?"

Maggie Flynn from Waterford had definitely outgrown her class. She had walked with kings and lost the common touch. This is not completely true because when the wine was flowing I occasionally saw glimpses of the lonely woman. Playing the piano on Monday nights she seemed to enter another world, her accent reverted to the soft tones of her home land and there were traces of the vulnerable colleen she had once been. Often tears streamed down her face as she lost herself in the music. Sometimes at the end of the evening, whilst still very ladylike she was unsteady on her feet. I had the job of making sure she got to her front door safely.

I was always respectful and called her Countess, she appreciated this in her grand manner and explained to me that her friends lacked culture, breeding and were sadly lacking in the social graces,

"Despite my best efforts Patrick, they will never appreciate the finer things of life."

REBECCA COLLINS

Cupid's arrows had quite a large target when they hit Rebecca. She was six foot tall and weighed in at twenty stone when she met Luigi. Luigi, damaged from the war and suffering with his nerves, tried to fight his demons and lost. He launched himself into eternity, a rope tied around his neck tied to a top floor banister; he left behind a very competent wife. She coped well with her two lodging houses and like a great sailing ship she paraded daily between her houses and the King's.

Her drains got blocked one holiday weekend and she sent a messenger to my lodgings to know if I could help. I had great misgivings but I went. I was greeted by an atrocious smell and the great Amazonian figure of Rebecca in full working regalia. Her face was red, she was sweating profusely and she looked enormous in a black boiler suit with McAlphine's logo proudly displayed on the back. To add to this ensemble she had pulled on a large pair of waders and wore red arm length gloves. I had a gut feeling that my weekend was completely cocked up.

"Thanks for coming Patrick. I have tried to rod but the rods got stuck. The council offices are shut and I really am in deep shit."

She asked one of her staff to make me some breakfast and this gave me some time to think. I noticed she had used up all the drain rods before they got stuck. It was obvious that the blockage was between the house and the sewer in the middle of the road and not in her backyard. Rebecca and I both knew this would attract some sightseers and idlers.

She was now beginning to get agitated and throw fucks at her long suffering staff. Luckily most of her lodgers were away for the weekend. She poured out two large measures of whiskey, and threw a gallon of Jeyes fluid over the pavement. She cursed the council, the Water Board, the local MPs and the governments of several countries. People held their noses as they passed by and when a kindly dog walker asked if I had some trouble, she barked, "No, he does this for fucking amusement!"

Most of her neighbours now showed interest in the proceedings. With a shovel borrowed from a neighbour, I had cleared away some of the debris from Rebecca's front garden and found the lid of an interceptor. When I examined this it was flooded, the smell was vile and there was no trace of the drain rods.

It was now middle day and despite the smell little groups of idlers were beginning to gather. I listened politely to all their advice and tried to reassure Rebecca. I had to get a pump to empty the pit to see what was going on. I did not have a driving licence and I needed a flat back lorry to fetch the pump from the works yard. Rebecca called her nephew in Harrow and he agreed to bring his lorry and help. During this period some public spirited souls had rung the Department of Health. Rebecca bristled when a well-dressed man stepped from a car and came over to have a look. He wore a sneer from ear to ear. He had built up shoes and wore a waistcoat and carried a clipboard,

"May I ask who owns this house?" he said fixing me with his piggy little eyes.

I ignored him and continued to contain the mess; I could see the little prick was revelling in our predicament. He drew himself up to his full height and said loudly, "I shall have to close these premises for the duration."

When Rebecca heard this she lost it completely. She grabbed the shovel from my hands and rushed at him swearing, "I do not need galvanised bastards like you. Fuck off back to your office, you superannuated wanker."

By now the bystanders sensed some street theatre and began to cheer. The man from the Department ran back to his car and locked himself in. A policeman arrived as if by magic and wanted to know why the crowd; why the disturbance;

what was causing the smell, and why I had not coned off the area. I had visions of another night in the cells and was a bundle of nerves. The policeman was an older man and stroking his chin listened to my explanation. Things seemed to be calming down and I think the copper was sympathetic, but then things are never that simple.

Unfortunately, Rebecca had a faint trace of a moustache on her upper lip and one of the little toe rags in the crowd asked if she had shaved that morning. After a day of aggravation Rebecca went loopy and hit him full in the façe. He fell in the midst of the sewage and when Rebecca took a swipe at another jeering bystander she lost her footing, grabbed the policeman to save herself and they both landed in the mess. He blew his whistle and in no time we had a Black Maria and half of Paddington's police force present.

Rebecca's nephew, with the flat back lorry, arrived just in time to see her and two scallywags being loaded into the police wagon. I was not arrested, as the policeman told his colleagues I was just a workman. When they left for the station the little ponce from the Department re-surfaced once more. He was much braver now and began to throw his weight around. He scribbled furiously in his notebook and quoted laws going back to the eighteenth century. I massaged his ego to the best of my ability and eventually convinced him that, seeing as he could not produce any shit shovellers over the weekend and as I was his best bet, he put up some danger notices and went home for his tea.

By this time I had cleared it with my boss and I could borrow a pump and some hoses. After collecting the pump from our yard, Rebecca's nephew went to the police station as he was worried about his aunt. He mentioned that she was quite well known there and that she was a regular source of worry to his mother. Luckily the pump worked and the level dropped. Rebecca's brute force had caused most of the trouble. I replaced the lid and tidied up.

The sun was sinking and the spectators were disappearing when Jimmy returned with his aunt. She was very subdued and smelt to high heaven. We returned the equipment to the yard and Rebecca said she would see us in the King's. Later Jimmy returned to his family, I went back to my lodgings to burn the slacks and shirt I had worn that day and spent ages trying to get clean.

A drunken Rebecca regaled the customers in the saloon bar that evening with all the dramas of the day. She praised my efforts and gave me five pounds. She was smelling sweeter than earlier and was in much better humour. We had a very pleasant evening but at the end had to dissuade Rebecca from going around to the police station and calling them a lot of silly bastards. There were no serious repercussions, after the events of the day. We heard no more from the Department of Health, Rebecca got a warning but avoided prosecution. The policeman and I were on first name terms. A fatherly figure, he told me to be careful of the company I kept. Peter Jones told all and sundry and I was now a member of the royal and ancient order of shit shovellers.

MARIA BARNES PUB LANDLADY

Marie Barnes came from a long line of innkeepers. "We were purveyors of wine and spirits dear, not just drunkards' labourers."

She loved the early mornings - the sun shining through the saloon bar windows, her pet cat stretching lazily before the freshly kindled fire; the highly polished bottles and glasses reflecting the dancing flames. The clip-clop of the drayman's horses, the withdrawal of bolts on the cellar door flap and then the sensuous thud of beer barrels thrown down on to well stuffed bales of straw. Most of all she loved to orchestrate the cleaner's activities, to open all the windows fully and eradicate the stale fumes of beer and tobacco from the previous night's excesses. A quick check on the tills' floats and she made the first pot of tea of the day and dispensed biscuits to her helpers. In half an hour she would draw the bolts and welcome her first customer.

Maria was liked by most people; she once told me that she gave her heart to many and her mind to few. She had a good sense of humour, a figure bordering on Rubenesque and was always immaculately dressed. She had pale features and jet black hair which she wore swept up in a bun. She wore severe black suits and always had three rows of white pearls. Her ample bosom, long finger nails painted a maroon colour, and shapely legs encased in seamed nylons made her seem sophisticated to boys of my age. She was happy with herself and had chosen the perfect profession. She could tailor her conversation to suit duke or dustman. She owned her pub and was reputed to have old money, but she was a source of great mystery to the ladies of W10. To their certain knowledge this well groomed, good looking woman had never had a man in her life. With the certainty of all gossips they were sure there had never been a woman in her life either.

Maria's flat was not accessible through the pub. It was on the fourth floor and had its own private entrance. It was so private that despite the best efforts of local know-alls, nobody but Maria had ever crossed the portals of her residence. She greeted trades folk and callers at the street door but they were never invited to climb the stairs. And so the wonder grew.

Her parents had bought her the pub but had never visited her there. She had bought a television to watch the Coronation but stopped the delivery man at the street door and had lugged the heavy TV up the stairs herself. Delivery boys were requested to call during pub opening hours and leave her shopping in the bar. She did not have a cleaning lady for her flat and gossip-in-chief Mrs Hill said it had not been decorated in living memory. "Must be like a council tip, my dear."

Imagination ran riot and people began to tell themselves stories. Was she hiding a criminal on the run? Did she practise some ancient religion? Was she hiding stolen goods? When questioned by the inquisitive how she spent her leisure hours, Maria always answered sweetly, "I have little time; I sleep, read and watch TV."

This never satisfied fevered minds and rumours grew more bizarre as the years rolled on.

Nobody considered that Maria spending sixteen hours a day with the public might require a little time and space for herself, but then the luxury of privacy was rare in W10.

Maria Barnes called me off the street one Saturday morning. "Have a drink, Patrick; I need your advice."

It was quite early and the barmen and cleaners kept glancing inquisitively. I felt really special when she poured two whiskeys and sat at a table with me. This was a first, even brewery reps were not invited to sit with Maria.

"Mrs Doyle tells me you do all her repairs now."

I told her that was correct. She replenished our whiskeys and puffed nervously on a cigarette. She was ill at ease and looked so serious when she said, "Patrick, I think I have a problem in my flat."

I remember joking, "Mrs Barnes, nothing is a problem that can be cured with a cheque book."

I felt she did not appreciate my flippancy. "Patrick, some mornings there is no water in the drinking water tap. I have checked with the water board and they have assured me the problem is internal. Have you got any ideas?"

"I will go up and have a look straight away, Mrs Barnes."

Her reaction could not have been more startling if I had asked her to strip. She shot to her feet. "No, No, Patrick, it may settle down; I do not want to put you to any trouble."

I was intrigued, as at this time I did not know how private Maria's flat was. I was also conscious that I could not diagnose a problem from a distance. I told Maria so and left the pub slightly puzzled.

Over the following weeks she kept me up to date on what proved to be an intermittent fault. I did quite a lot of the pub maintenance. One morning I noticed Maria filling water bottles in the bar and at the risk of being snubbed I volunteered to check the water in her flat.

"Mrs Barnes the drawings show a pipe line float switch in the duct in your kitchen; I think this may be the cause of the trouble."

She gazed at me. "Patrick, can you be completely sure?"

Patience was never one of my strong points and I knew Mrs Barnes was a competent, clued in lady, so I felt the time had come for some straight talking. "Mrs Barnes, I can enter your kitchen from the back fire escape, remove the duct panels and examine what I suspect. I promise a speedy conclusion and I will keep dust and mess to a minimum."

By now a bit of ego had crept into my feelings and I wanted to put this job to bed. She lit a cigarette and gazed at me speculatively. "I must admit I want it resolved as I am pissed off collecting drinking water from the bar."

I had the distinct feeling that she had to consult with somebody close to her, but who was the oracle?

She called at my lodgings on Friday evening and Mrs Doyle welcomed her like royalty.

"Kathleen, I need Patrick over the weekend if that is possible, he is looking at a problem in my flat." We agreed that I would start the next morning; I would knock at the fire escape door and go where no other man had gone before.

When Maria left I began to plan for the job as if it was a military exercise. Mrs Doyle thought it was hilarious and kept asking me if I felt apprehensive. She jokingly said I should write down my last wishes and my parent's address.

The buzz in the saloon bar that night could not have been greater if I was about to climb Everest. Peter Jones remarked, "Patrick, I hear her ladyship is lowering the drawbridge tomorrow." Everybody knew everything on the Harrow Road.

I climbed the fire escape next morning looking forward to the great adventure. I knocked and Maria opened the door. She was fully dressed despite the earliness of the hour. "I am impressed Patrick, right on time."

The kitchen was spotless; I was quite pleased that Mrs Hill, the queen gossip, had got that bit wrong. As I worked Maria stood guard in front of her living room door. She seemed interested in the proceedings. Once finished I cleared up and made my way to the fire escape exit, and Maria went to get her handbag. She was glad we were finished before opening hours and wanted to pay me. During the opening and closing of the living room door I spotted a smart camel hair overcoat and a pair of shiny black men's shoes. I carried my tools to the bottom of the fire escape and despite skilful questioning from the ladies of W10, Mrs Barnes secret remained just that.

JOAN HAYES

Mrs Joan Hayes enjoyed being miserable, and at times I worked for her. I found her gloominess contagious, she was also aggressive when drunk and that I found hard to deal with. I found it hard to avoid her as she had a never-ending list of maintenance jobs in her house. The first time I came in contact with her she was rubbishing her husband in the King's. "He is the laziest bastard the Lord ever put breath in; fell out with work ten years ago. Bad back, my Irish arse, it's just that he can't get it off the bed." At seventeen, it was the first time that I was aware that not all marriages are made in heaven. I had a romantic view of everything up to that point.

The corners of her mouth drooped, her lips curled and she showed her teeth when she got hostile. Of medium height and build, with short blonde hair and a pale complexion, she wore leopard print dresses and occasionally looked as if she was going to bite your head off. The saloon bar of the King's was her platform on Monday nights. Her friends usually told her to shut up and listen to the music. She'd then sulk for the remainder of the evening. Molly Ryan used to try to get her to lighten up, pointing out that anything was better in bed than a vacant space.

The second time I saw Joan she had just stepped out of the bath, to let me in. Paddy had not been able to get his back off the bed that morning and she was in a vile mood. "When I threw that bastard out of my bed, I should have thrown him on the street."

I had a couple of hours work on her boiler; she stayed with me in her bath towel, keeping up a steady stream of abuse at Paddy.

"Spoilt by his mother he was; she had his socks warmed in the oven before he changed them. Convinced him he wasn't strong and that his weak back was hereditary. Fell for him like a ton of bricks I did, he was always like a new pin and he had lovely teeth. We married at the start of the war and his bad back kept him out of the army. Men were scarce then and I suppose he was the best that was about. His mother stayed with us till two in the morning on our wedding night. She warned him against helping in the kitchen, told him it was women's work. Kept on about his position in the town hall and how taxing that was on his back sitting behind a desk in reception and pointing people in the right direction. Even that got too much for him and he hasn't had a job in six years."

I felt embarrassed but she seemed to get enjoyment from her ranting and raving and glared at me as if daring me to disagree with her. I pushed on with the job and was quite relieved when the time came to light the fire. I then had an hour to wait so I could check my work. She poured out two large glasses of whiskey and when Paddy heard the clink of glasses he suddenly came to life and emerged from the bedroom.

Paddy stood six feet tall. He had iron grey hair and a swarthy complexion. He had gleaming white teeth and a pencil moustache. He had soft hands like a diplomat and with his ornate dressing gown and carpet slippers he looked like a gentleman of leisure. He gazed at Joan. "Why are you undressed woman? I suppose you have used the last of the hot water."

I chipped in to tell him there would be heaps of hot water in an hour. He looked at me disdainfully, avoiding eye contact. He poured himself a glass of whiskey and told Joan to fetch his cigarettes from the bedroom. To my great surprise she meekly obeyed. He told her to get dressed and she scuttled off. In her absence he gazed into space and on her return ordered her to lay out his clothes and run his bath. I hurriedly began to collect my tools. I was quite shaken and deeply embarrassed. Just before I left she asked him if he wanted a cooked breakfast. "Just toast and marmalade, my dear; thick slices with plenty of butter. Oh, by the way, I suppose sex is out of the question?"

I felt this was for my benefit; I grabbed my tools and ran from these strange people.

One week later she tried to kill Paddy. Luckily one of her lodgers arrived back from his holidays that Monday morning, because Joan was at the bag wash. He found Paddy unconscious at the bottom of the stairs. He alerted the emergency services and Paddy was taken to St. Mary's. It was touch and go for a fortnight but then he came out of the coma. He had several broken ribs, a dislocated shoulder and a severe bump on the back of the head. Joan stayed at his bedside weeping and praying for his recovery. The police showed interest but when Paddy got his senses back his memories of the incident had vanished. He told the police that due to his bad back he was unsteady on his feet and must have fallen down the stairs and bumped his head. The policeman wrote 'domestic' in his notebook and never bothered him again.

Dustmen took away a three legged coffee table from the Hayes house that week. All the legs could be unscrewed and one leg was never found. Joan had Paddy's bedroom re-decorated, she bought him a new orthopaedic mattress and a wardrobe of new clothes. She gazed at him adoringly when he was discharged, and presented him with an expensive walking cane, as he now walked with a pronounced limp.

His demands increased when he came home: a new radio and television, his own bottle of Dimple Haig and breakfast in bed. He was also reading a lot so she had to visit the library every week, sometimes twice, as the books she chose were not to his taste. Joan got skinnier and she whined and moaned to those that would listen.

Unfortunately I was given the position of chief listener as there was a never ending flow of work from her house. When Paddy informed her that due to lack of exercise he would now need physiotherapy and massage she engaged a Miss Drew from Praed Street to minister to him three times a week. She told me that Paddy spoke highly of her healing hands.

Miss Henrietta Drew or Miss Lazarus, as she was known to her colleagues, was slim and athletic. She travelled to her clients on a bicycle with high handlebars. She charged one guinea per session and took customers on recommendation only. Three times a week, complete with black bag, she entered the Hayes' household. She was given her own key as Joan was at the bag wash on Mondays. Her treatment made unbelievable improvements on Paddy's back. In fact it was miraculous because when Joan returned unexpectedly one Monday lunchtime she found Paddy lying on the orthopaedic mattress with a flushed Miss Lazarus astride him and he vigorously massaging the small of her back. Joan went for her with a mop handle. Henrietta disengaged herself, dressed, grabbed her black bag and left the Hayes' household not even stopping to collect her fee.

Joan told everyone in the King's that evening and at the end told a hushed audience, "The lazy bastard has now found out that he can have sex without ever getting his back off the bed."

Her friends were at their most ladylike and greeted this revelation with gasps of amazement. Molly Ryan was probably the most knowledgeable in these matters and she soon piped up, "Of course it's possible to do it standing or lying and if you had wings you could do it flying."

Joan changed over the next few weeks. She still rubbished Paddy on Monday nights but her heart wasn't in it. She had this dreamy, far-away look in her eyes. The harsh lines around her mouth began to soften and she was beginning to dress with care. She put on a stone, visited the hairdresser weekly and began to attract wolf whistles when she passed our workshop door. Now with high heels, short skirts and lipstick applied in a cupid's bow she was positively sexy. Then one Monday night she asked the Countess to play something romantic. Sam the Eel almost choked on his cigar when she sidled over and tried to sit on his knee. By the end of the next day every gossip on the Harrow Road had jaw ache. The following Sunday on her way from church an American serviceman was seen attending to the clasp of pearls she wore.

Molly Ryan told me that she could always tell if a woman was fulfilled. "Shows on the face, Patrick. I swear she's having it off; I wish I knew who the man was."

I kept my own council and never told her that Warring and Gillow had delivered a king size bed to the Hayes' household and Joan had given the orthopaedic mattress to the St. Vincent de Paul Society.

Paddy and Joan were now often seen arm in arm in Golborne Road, and Miss Lazarus still pedalled her bicycle through the streets of Paddington; with her black bag and cheeky smile she was the fore runner of our present day chiropractors.

HELENA BROWN

If Helena Brown had never met Ted while shopping in Portobello Road and if they had never had a damp patch under their dado rail, I would never have crossed their threshold and avoided a lot of trouble and aggravation. Despite the fact that Ted had been a painter and decorator before marriage, Helena had relegated him to house husband and he spent most of his time in the kitchen. He was in fact the first man I had ever seen wearing an apron and rubber gloves. This regalia combined with a tweed cap, with grey locks wrapping around the brim made him appear like something from a Punch and Judy show.

I got bad feelings about that job from the start. Then Helena was Mrs Doyle's best friend and at that time she had a lot of influence over me. Helena was a very assertive woman and when I told her she probably needed a builder she glared and said she had every confidence in me.

"Ted says it's not rising damp as there are no signs of it in the basement."

Ted had started his career as a tea boy on the building sites. A mild mannered likable man, and with the shortage of labour during the war, he had drifted into the trade. He married in his early twenties and his young brother, who disliked work, came to live with the young couple. Shortly after his brother ran away with his wife, he then resumed a bachelor existence until he was captured by Helena in the market place.

From the outset she took charge. There was a will of iron under her soft curves. She was tall with slightly bowed legs and hair worn tightly in a bun. When she eye-balled Ted she had a predatory look and you felt he was being dissected. He had a thin scrawny neck and shirt collars always appeared six sizes too big for him. He was always spotless except for a ring of dandruff on his coat collar. Helena ordered him to assist me in every way and then read him the riot act when the beds weren't changed. Despite my dust sheets, when I removed the sodden wallpaper he fussed around me with a dust pan and brush. She sat on the stairs and I think by this time she had realised that I had no magic wand in my tool box.

I was now convinced that a lead pipe embedded in the wall was the cause of the problem. With an icy feeling in my stomach I realised it was a demolition job to get to it and affect a repair. Matters were further complicated as Helena shared a party wall with her neighbours the Lazio family. They had not been on speaking terms since the war. When I told Helena of the need to remove her highly varnished dado rail and make an exploratory hole in the wall she reached for the whiskey bottle. She took a large swig and neglected to offer Ted or me any. She gave me permission to proceed.

It was late in the afternoon when I located the leak. It was a couple of inches away from breaking into the Lazio's hallway and the water was coming from their rising main. I now had a barrow load of bricks and plaster taken out of the Brown's hallway, and with a sinking feeling I realised there would be an international incident. I marshalled my thoughts and told Helena of my findings. I carefully explained that her neighbours were not to blame. Helena knew better. Despite being second generation Irish she was no great lover of immigrants. I told her that before I could continue I would have to contact the Lazio family. That was difficult in itself as three generations of the family were out in their ice-cream vans from morning to night. Helena was now half pissed as she had been sipping whiskey all that afternoon. Ted gazed sadly at the leak, sucked on a woodbine and cracked his fingers. There was an air of tension.

Helena piped up, "I will talk to that bloody lot when they get back."

I pleaded with her as I felt I was in a better position to aid these international affairs.

With the sun setting and the moon lying on its back, three van load of Lazio's swept into the street. There was a lot of noise and chatter, as the leader of the clan gave them all instruction. Juan Lazio was in his sixties, iron grey hair, stockily built and wearing a spotless white t-shirt. He had bangles on his wrists and a gold medallion hung from a chain around his neck. He was tanned and muscular and a livid scar ran from his left eye to the tip of his chin. He drank on his own in the King's and Sam the Eel referred to him as the Don. I was in a worse state of nerves than Ted by then. The Don's wife stood by his side. She was a thick set woman dressed in black. She had perspiration marks on her dress and tufts of hair peeped out from her armpits. The rest of the tribe handed the Don the day's takings and vanished into the house.

Helena was in the back room and heard the racket. She rushed out onto the street. Unfortunately Ted wasn't fast enough to get out of her way. She bumped against him and his long white apron got tangled between his legs. He was sent hurling down the front step. Helena did not bother to pick him up but with all her lack of diplomacy confronted the Don. Poor Ted sat on the steps nursing what later proved to be a broken collar bone.

"Why don't you fuck off back to Italy; your poxy lead pipes are spraying water into my hallway."

The Don was at a disadvantage. He stared at her disdainfully and then appealed to Ted, "Why don't you control this stupid woman?"

Ted gazed at Helena like a rabbit in the headlights and I stood shivering in the night air.

My mind was racing as Helena and the Don exchanged insults. Helena was at last persuaded to attend to Ted, as moaning pitifully he slumped sideways on the step. She went inside to ring an ambulance and the Don and his wife went indoors.

I was left with the leak and a need to get into the Lazio's hallway. The ambulance arrived and the Brown's left for the hospital. With the moon now high in the sky I was alone. Lover's walked home, arms entwined, sounds of revelry from a late night party drifted over the rooftops towards me. I cursed Helena; I was tired and hungry and began to question my place in these international negotiations. Despondent, I kept emptying the tray which kept filling with water and looked to God for guidance.

At midnight the Don opened his door to walk his dog. With his Alsatian and black leather coat, he looked like Gestapo. I resolved to try to reason with him. "Excuse me, Mr Lazio, I need to repair a leak and can only do so from your hallway."

"You're Patrick from the King's aren't you? Mrs Doyle, your mother no? Why you work for this mad woman? She perhaps not pay you?"

I neglected to tell him that Helena felt he would have to pay for the damage in her hall. I just wanted to stop the leak and go home.

"Will it cause damage to my hall?" I explained the ramifications. The Alsatian growled impatiently.

The Don made up his mind, opened the door and thankfully put the dog in the back room. When I had finished, the Don made coffee and sandwiches. He had gone up in my estimation.

"Mr Brown needs to control that stupid tart he calls a wife." With a sigh of relief I bade him goodnight.

I returned the next day. Ted had his arm in a sling and Helena was in a foul mood as she had just copped that Ted's household duties were compromised with only one arm. I told her I had fixed the leak so I would make good and tidy the mess,

"You may as well, seeing as they will be footing the bill in any case."

I repaired both hallways and made my way to the King's to wash the taste of a terrible episode out of my mouth.

I eventually got paid from both parties but only on condition that I told neither. International disputes were unresolved and I had the spoils of war.

DOT DUNNE

The rain battered the window pane and the Paddington canal was a dirty, brownish colour. Street lights were beginning to pierce the darkness. Late night shoppers huddled at the bus stops, occasionally diving for cover as buses splashed through the rain soaked streets.

Dot Dunne's knitting had fallen from her grasp. She was snoring gently as her cat stared into the embers of a dead fire. She had missed Saturday night theatre on the radio once again. She worked every Saturday afternoon changing beds with Mrs Doyle. She was always exhausted on completing the twenty-eight beds. She woke with a start at eleven, set the clock for six, fed the cat and crawled into bed.

Tomorrow she would travel to Lewes prison to see young Tony. The following Sunday she would travel to Reading Gaol to see her husband. Dot said her prayers and turned off the light. Sleep gave respite from the sadness she carried around. Paying her bills was an on-going struggle. Chain smoking had given her a weak chest. She had varicose veins and fallen arches, these added to her aggravations, and whiskey was now playing a part in her life.

Dot was in service with an English family when she met Jimmy Dunne. He was a good looking, two bit con man, who would later progress to becoming a full time member of the criminal fraternity. He had a nice flat in Maida vale and drove a car, when flashing car keys in a dance hall in the thirties was a big plus. They married quickly and Jimmy impressed the naive young Irish girl. He promised her heaven and gave her hell. He'd managed to convince her he was a legitimate business man. These were the early days before he was known by the police. Tony was born within the year. Dot began to notice a great shortage of money. Jimmy was always owed, expecting or promised money. In the meantime Dot had to take cleaning jobs to put food on the table.

Being naive, she spoke of the jewels on the dressing table of one of the ladies she cleaned for. Two nights later they disappeared. There was no sign of breaking or entering. With the owner's away and Dot the possessor of keys, she found herself in the police station. Luckily they believed her when she denied all knowledge of the robbery. Her world collapsed when she went home, found Jimmy gone and her young infant in the care of a neighbour.

The shades really fell from her eyes when Jimmy arrived back after a fortnight, broke and apologetic. He was arrested twenty-four hours later and sentenced to two years. He had spent the proceeds of the robbery in West End spielers. In quick succession Dot lost her cleaning jobs and the flat in Maida Vale. Putting her only child with a child minder she got a factory job and a flat in Westbourne Park.

Mrs Doyle became her friend and helped her through the bad times. Dot believed in marrying for better and for worse. She often borrowed money to visit Jimmy whilst he was at the pleasure of her majesty. He still had grandiose money making schemes but Dot had lost some of her greenness. On his release from prison he persuaded Isodore Green that he wanted to make good and learn a trade. Dot did some cleaning in Isodore's shop and she pleaded for him.

Mr Green, a kindly man, said, "I know he has done some sewing Dorothy, please God he has seen the light."

Jimmy's skills honed from sewing prison mail bags did not allow the light to shine. He took liberties and stole a bale of expensive cloth. Mr Green gave him two options, police or pack in. He left immediately, robbed a factory in Acton and went back to prison. Prison visits with her young son became a way of life for Dot. Despite her best efforts Tony grew up to be a tear away and graduated from petty theft to robbing banks and post offices. The CID were now frequent visitors to Dot's.

Dot kept the home together and welcomed both husband and son on prison releases. They dragged her down and she always refused to take money from them. They were flush occasionally and liked to cut a dash in the saloon bar. It was always short lived as the police were aware of their scams. Sam the Eel said they gave local villains a bad name. Maria Barnes banned them from the pub. They tried to make an issue of it but they quickly retreated when Sam eye-balled them through a haze of cigar smoke.

Dot did the pools, I sometimes fetched her a three shilling postal order. Every Tuesday she posted her coupon marked with an X for no publicity. She and millions like her hoped for a miracle; odds similar to being struck by lightning. When I asked her if she studied form, she laughed, "I just put down some numbers and if God wills it, I am bound to win."

Jimmy and Tony were starting long sentences, five and four years respectively, when Dot won nineteen thousand pounds. She called to see Kathleen on Sunday evening, trembling all over. Her face was red, she was wheezing and she fortified herself with a whiskey. Kathleen poured her another, we checked her coupon, she had eight draws.

We were really delighted for her and we promised to keep her secret. She was able to pack in her job with Kathleen as the stairs were getting too much for her. That kind of money was sufficient for her simple needs and she resolved not to tell her husband or son about her new found wealth.

Money gave Dot a new lease of life. She could now buy the latest fashions from the good shops and avoid her usual jumble sales. She now wore smart spectacles and the old ones shrouded in sticking plaster were binned. Her speech improved as she was able to replace her old clicking dentures. Her varicose veins were operated on in a small private hospital in Hammersmith. After thirty-five years she was able to holiday in Ireland and look up some of her relatives. On her return she was unsettled, went back and bought a house with a garden, a few miles from her birth place.

I visited Dot in the seventies. She was now an old lady. The haunted look had left her face. She kept a few chickens and was very proud of her flower and vegetable garden. It was as if her husband and son had never existed. She never mentioned them, but she exchanged letters with her old friend Mrs Doyle.

THE THRESHOLD

By 1955 I found I could now afford to rest on Sundays. It was sheer luxury. I began to take stock of where I was living and began to explore the great city of London. Tea dances in the Bamba in Kilburn High Street were now the highlight of my week and I found it refreshing to mix with people of my own age group. Being asked where you came from seemed to start off most conversation. The dance halls played a very big part in my life for a while and helped to dispel a lot of loneliness.

I was approaching the end of my apprenticeship and my mind was a medley of hopes and dreams. Political meetings in draughty halls were beginning to lose their attraction; if Shelia from Derry was not there to inspire me, I think my attendances would have been sporadic. I was not a great fan of capitalism at that time but I began to get a gut feeling that communism would not answer all the frailties of the human race. I told Shelia about my misgivings, she was very committed, so when I told her that I felt both 'isms' lead to the same crass materialism, she told me to unload all the spiritual crap and move on. She reiterated the old saws about religion being the opium of the poor and it was time for me to break away from the stranglehold of the Catholic Church. I told her this would not be an option; it led to many late night debates. She was a cradle Catholic, like me, but had formed the opinion that especially in her native city religions had proved divisive and split the strength of the working classes of both persuasions.

My years on the Harrow Road were drawing to a close; I had mixed feelings. Despite bouts of loneliness, I had grown to like my new friends. The struggle for survival was not as intense and I found with my increased wages I could now relax a little. I began to live a little. On Sundays I dressed with care and smothered with after shave and Brilliantine made my way to the Bamba. This was an Irish dance hall. It was all very proper; girls and boys stood at opposite sides of the hall and you declared how serious you were when you asked a girl to have tea and biscuits. Girls had to be especially careful because some mean spirited boys felt that if a girl said yes, for the outlay of seven pence, they would be transported to heaven that night.

It was usually considered advisable to have some lessons at The Court School of Dancing before frequenting the dance halls. The teachers all wore penguin suits and hair parted in the middle. The female teachers were all beautifully mannered, very sophisticated and usually just a tiny bit snooty, probably to compensate for having their toes walked on from time to time.

Irish dance halls, at that time, played a big role in the social life of thousands of young emigrants. Show bands were plentiful and of very good quality. The walls were decorated with Irish scenic views and were very evocative.

Romances blossomed in those halls in the fifties, and when dancing finished it was considered swish to invite a lady to a very smart cocktail bar on Kilburn High Road. It was called the American Bar; it now welcomed all nations as the Yankee servicemen were returning home.

Shelia was now a fully trained nurse and shortly after got a job in Belfast. We were quite sad when we parted, and with all the intensity of teenagers, promised undying love and friendship. We never met again but I did read about her in the seventies. She was still attempting to bring about change. I am glad I knew her, this warm, compassionate girl from Derry. I hoped she would always keep that fire in her belly, as we so badly need radicals as most of us lose it as we become old and fat.

I will always be grateful to Jock McLarren and Bill May for the help they gave me and the pains they took to make sure I turned out a reasonable engineer. Bill made sure I took pride in my work, to admit when I got it wrong and to never gloss over a bad job. The pipe smoking Jock told me to always treat customer's money as if it was my own. When Jock told me I had passed my City and Guilds and organised the banging out ceremony in the workshop, I felt it had all been worthwhile. My workmates plied me with whiskey and light ale, and I was presented with a kit of tools and a wallet with twenty pounds. I felt quite tearful that day as I knew there would soon be a parting of the ways.

The landladies gave me what they termed a send-off on the Monday night before I left the Harrow Road. For one reason or another it was to be almost fifty years before I returned there. Memories of that evening still bring a lump to my throat despite the intervening years. Sam the Eel's mother, in all her Romany finery, had entered the King's for the first time in her life. Helena Brown had dragged her hen pecked husband to the do. She wore a fur coat and Ted looked smart in a blue suit. His collar was still too big. He stood miserably, on his own, drinking halves of mild and bitter. Widow Jones arrived with her new squeeze, a retired bus conductor from Birmingham, who gazed around apprehensively. Mrs Jones was slightly the worse for wear and teetering on her high heels. He had to reach out frequently and grab the back of her whale bone corset to prevent her from stumbling. Countess Heggar, petite and ladylike, was sitting at the piano, shuffling her music and staring down her nose at us lesser mortals. She sipped gin and Italian daintily and played *Moore's Melodies* from time to time. All twenty stone of Rebecca Collins arrived. She divested herself of a huge fur coat and for some reason handed it to Ted Brown. Helena took umbrage.

"Do you think he's a bloody cloak room attendant?"

Maria Barnes diffused the situation, smiled sweetly and hung it out the back. Ted cracked his fingers nervously and lit up a woodbine.

Paddy and Joan Hayes arrived late. She told anyone that would listen that they had taken to going to bed in the afternoon and had overslept. Rebecca mentioned that she had seen Miss Lazarus in the week. Maria stepped in at that moment to congratulate the duo on how well they looked.

The party was a great success. Maria Barnes was a wonderful hostess. She circulated, kept glasses topped up and seemed to have an uncanny knack of stepping in where there might be dissension. Agnes Glynn was in her element. She sang the old songs with depth and feeling. Sam the Eel sang *The Road to Mandalay* in a whiskey cracked tenor, and his mother played some haunting gypsy melodies on her violin. Kathleen Doyle sang *Danny Boy* and Ted Brown, now well fortified with ale, recited *Gunga Din*. He really came out of his shell and followed on with *The Green Eye of the little Yellow God*.

Most parties reach a crescendo and then slowly tail off. At two in the morning, fuelled by lots of alcohol, the noise was horrendous. The local policeman acting on complaints called. Maria invited him in and gave him a large whiskey in exchange for his lecture. We promised better behaviour and he departed, honour satisfied. We broke up at dawn and because of my alcohol consumption, probably for the first time I was excused escort duties. Widow Jones had been put to bed earlier and her escort was snoring gently in the corner. The Countess had convinced herself she was sober until she fell over outside. Helena Brown was telling Ted of her disgust at the amount he had drunk whilst unable to get off her own chair. Ted went outside to hail a taxi and walked into a lamp post. He was rescued by an early morning barrow boy and deposited back into the saloon bar.

It all gets a little hazy after that. I recall crossing the canal bridge with Kathleen Doyle in the early morning sunshine. Milk floats were whirring, the buses running, barrow boys were shouting and as we tottered down Kensal Green, the Harrow Road was coming alive.

NOSTALGIA

The sights, sounds and smells of Harrow Road in the mid-fifties are things I have never forgotten. Fifty years on they are for the memory only as they have disappeared or been superseded. Red double decker buses, pristine clean and manned by a driver and conductor, whizzed by frequently. The crew were immaculate, smart uniforms and ties and very seldom running late. Side roads uncluttered by cars. Grocer shops on most corners, mostly owned by stocky, prosperous Welshmen, they all delivered big or small orders by bicycle. Astute and conscientious men they were always on time and were on first name terms with their customers. They employed delivery boys and the bikes had huge baskets always piled high, pedalling at break neck speed, ringing their bells.

Whole pigs and lambs hung in the butcher shops. Each butcher had a chopping block and prepared individual orders from the carcase, whacking great sides of meat on the chopping board with sharp knives flashing. The customers got individual attention.

Greengrocer's worked from barrows, shouting loudly they were found on most street corners. They went to Covent Garden or Brentford early in the mornings, brought in their stock and took great care with their displays. Transactions were cash only.

The first sound of the morning was the whirring of the milk floats and the clinking of milk bottles. All houses had deliveries, fridges largely non-existent and fresh milk was a must, especially for infants.

There was no over-lapping of trades. Newsagents and tobacconists were just that. They kept within their remits and only became largely extinct with the advent of supermarkets.

Street newspaper sellers were a law unto themselves. They usually started work at mid-day and their shout of '*Star*, *News* and *Standard*' was heard on most corners. Wonderful entrepreneurs, they doubled up as bookmakers before the advent of betting shops.

Rag and bone men were also part of the scene. They trawled the streets with shouts of "Any old iron", the slow clip-clop of the horses and shouts of the owners and the metallic din of all kinds of scrap. Sometimes on their own, often in pairs, they now seem to have vanished completely.

Coal was the main fuel and the delivery trolleys were always on the streets. The trolleys were horse drawn and when an order was shouted from a customer, the horses stopped without guidance. Coalmen wore old sacks on their heads and shoulders; it was a filthy job especially on wet days. Coal was delivered through houses and down to basement coal houses. The coalmen took care to avoid damage to the hallways but disputes were frequent.

Most pubs had jellied eel stalls outside; they were always popular and served up fresh bread with the eels, whelks and winkles. On Sunday evenings they pushed their barrows through the back streets and winkles were sold by the pint.

There were weekly visits to the cinema; TV had not taken over our lives and our living rooms. Home laundries were uncommon and the local bag wash was a vital service. They usually had bath houses attached where hot baths were always available. Each cubicle had a large bath, a back scrubber and a square of red carbolic soap. A bath towel was supplied when you paid your sixpence. It was not luxurious but supplied a need when great numbers of the population did not have bathrooms. The laundry with its huge, industrial washing machines, colanders and heated rollers made it possible to wash and dry in one day.

Monday was wash day for the ladies of W10. When the lodgers had been served breakfast, a great swarm of ladies set forth, with two wheeled wicker baskets piled high with up to one hundred sheets, these ladies went to wash their dirty laundry in public. It was a back breaking chore.

Lodgers fended for themselves on Monday evenings. This was the ladies day off. Food had been left available. The lodgers and ladies mutually respected each other's hard work. Things followed a pattern, lodgers celebrated on Saturdays and the ladies got well pissed on Mondays. When the last sheet had been ironed on the big rollers, celebrations began. Usually ten or twelve strong they trundled their baskets to the King's where they had the first of many drinks. Maria enjoyed the Monday ritual. With arms folded and large breasts resting on the bar she listened to the gossip. Maria had a lot in common with the group. They were all liberated before it was heard of. They were mostly widows or divorcees and made a good living without any help from a man. They shunned motor cars, foreign holidays and expensive clothes; all these ladies were cash rich. Tax laws were not very strict in the fifties and none of their income went to fancy accountants. It was not unusual for those ladies to have a whip round for a deserving cause on the Harrow Road.

Pubs closed at three and the ladies, leaving laundry baskets, moved on to the Green Door Club, which never closed. Jack Doyle, singer, actor, boxer and all round ladies' man held court there. Known in the tabloids as the Gorgeous Gael, he was visited there by his ex-wife, the Mexican actress Movita. She brought along a young American actor called Marlon Brando. Despite rubbing shoulders with celebrities, the ladies always went back to the King's at opening time and Maria always greeted them with large plates of sandwiches. Well lubricated, they let their hair down and enjoyed the rest of the evening.

The cider house served great numbers of people on the bottom rung of the drinking classes. It was a sad, dilapidated building. The sign said Conner's Cider House. It had rough deal tables and stools stained with cider and charred from forgotten cigarettes. The wine of the west was popular and cheap. This bar was frequented by great numbers teetering on the verge of alcoholism.

Fish and chip shops were everywhere before the advent of curry and kebab shops. On freezing, foggy nights, when the pubs closed, they were usually the next port of call. The smell of frying fish with plenty of salt and vinegar was a gastronomic treat. It was to be eaten in the open air and from a copy of yesterday's *Times*.

Last but not least, there was the church. It was on the next street to the King's. It was open from dawn to dusk without fear from vandals, always packed on Sundays, a time to talk to God and gossip with neighbours.

This was the Harrow Road of my teens. You could eat, drink, bet, pray and even get arrested, all within a quarter of a mile.

***

Lightning Source UK Ltd.
Milton Keynes UK
UKOW04f1607300814

237796UK00002B/5/P